"Stay here tonight, Jana."

Her stomach flip-flopped. "But I don't *know* you."

"I think you know what matters. I need to find my daughters. Tell me you don't think staying here will help."

She knew better than he did that she could tune into the girls' energy more easily surrounded by their possessions. "I can't."

His blue eyes darkened, his head lowered almost imperceptibly, but enough that his face was slightly closer to hers. He paused for a moment, then raised his head. They both knew if he kissed her, she wouldn't stay the night—and she might not return at all.

Dear Reader,

Babies—who can resist them? Celebrating the wonder of new life—and new love—Silhouette Romance introduces a brand-new series, BUNDLES OF JOY. In these wonderful stories, couples are brought together by babies—and kept together by love! We hope you enjoy all six BUNDLES OF JOY books in April. Look for more in the months to come.

Favorite author Suzanne Carey launches the series with *The Daddy Project*. Sherry Tompkins is caring for her infant nephew and she needs help from the child's father, Mike Ruiz. Is marrying Mike the best way to find out if he's daddy material?

Lindsay Longford brings us *The Cowboy, the Baby and the Runaway Bride*. T. J. Tyler may have been left at the altar years ago by Callie Jo Murphy, but now this rugged cowboy and his adorable baby boy are determined to win her back.

Lullaby and Goodnight is a dramatic new story from Sandra Steffen about a single mom on the run. LeAnna Chadwick longs to stay in the shelter of Vince Macelli's arms, but the only way to protect her child is to leave the man she loves.

The excitement continues with *Adam's Vow*, Karen Rose Smith's book about one man's search for his missing daughters—and the beautiful, mysterious woman who helps him. Love and laughter abound in Pat Montana's *Babies Inc.*, a tale of two people who go into the baby business together and find romance in the process. And debut author Christine Scott brings us the heartwarming *Hazardous Husband*.

I hope you will enjoy BUNDLES OF JOY. Until next month—

Happy Reading!

Anne Canadeo
Senior Editor
Silhouette Romance

Please address questions and book requests to:
Silhouette Reader Service
U.S.: 3010 Walden Ave., P.O. Box 1325, Buffalo, NY 14269
Canadian: P.O. Box 609, Fort Erie, Ont. L2A 5X3

ADAM'S VOW

Karen Rose Smith

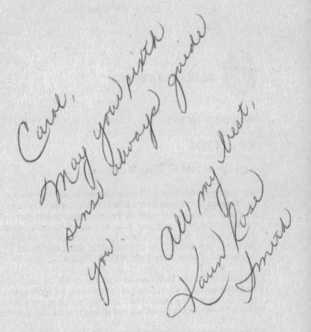

Carol,
May your sixth
sense always guide
you. All my best,
Karen Rose
Smith

Silhouette
R O M A N C E™
Published by Silhouette Books
America's Publisher of Contemporary Romance

To Sis and Bern,
who helped care for our bundle of joy.
Sis, thank you.
Bern, we miss you.

 SILHOUETTE BOOKS

ISBN 0-373-19075-1

ADAM'S VOW

This edition published by arrangement with Harlequin Enterprises B.V.

® and TM are trademarks of Harlequin Enterprises B.V., used under
license. Trademarks indicated with ® are registered in the United States
Patent and Trademark Office, the Canadian Trade Marks Office and in
other countries.

Printed in U.S.A.

Books by Karen Rose Smith

Silhouette Romance

Adam's Vow #1075

Silhouette Special Edition

Abigail and Mistletoe #930

Previously published under the pseudonym Kari Sutherland

Silhouette Romance

Heartfire, Homefire #973

Silhouette Special Edition

Wish On The Moon #741

*Darling Daddies

KAREN ROSE SMITH

lives in Hanover, Pennsylvania, with her husband, an elementary school librarian, and their son, a recent college graduate. Karen has read romances since she was a teenager precisely because they end with happily ever afters. She thinks everyone needs an escape from time to time. And a long time to come. She's thrilled to be writing under her real name for Silhouette. She formerly wrote under pseudonym Kari Sutherland. Readers can write to Karen at P.O. Box 1545, Hanover, PA 17331.

Dear Readers,

When I look at my son, I see the infant my husband and I brought home from the hospital; I feel the touch of his hand his first day of kindergarten; I remember the discussions we had as he journeyed through adolescence; I marvel that he is now a college graduate. All the feelings, tears and laughter live in my heart, and I will cherish them always.

Motherhood changed me and taught me my weaknesses and strengths. Fatherhood for my hero, Adam, has shown him his own weaknesses and strengths. His daughters teach him about love—what he has to do to nurture it. Although Adam doesn't realize it when he first seeks help to find his missing daughters, he is ready to share his life with a woman as well as with his children. As Jana, the heroine, helps reunite Adam with his girls, his "bundles of joy" forge a bond between the couple.

I am delighted to be included in this special month. Working with children in romances reminds me how much I miss my "baby," but how much I treasure my adult son. May this book bring back memories for my readers, may it touch their lives with joy.

With warm regards,

Karen Rose Smith

Prologue

Don't answer it.
Don't answer it.
Do not answer it.

Jana Kellerhern convinced herself to ignore the intrusive sound of the ringing telephone as the golden L.A. sun swept through her open living room window, along with the balmy June breeze.

Her phone rang a second time.

Plucking the leather-bound volumes from her bookshelf one by one, she dusted them with a soft cloth. She always cleaned and straightened her surroundings when her heart or mind was in turmoil. With a quick glance at the phone on her end table, she knew her mother wouldn't be calling on a Monday evening. Madge Kellerhern called her daughter from Deep River, Indiana, every Sunday at exactly 7:00 p.m.

Jana's phone rang a third time.

She swiped the cloth across the shelf, back and forth. In the three months since she'd relocated to L.A., she hadn't confided in anyone or encouraged close friendships. She needed this respite. She needed to find out whether her "gift" would continue to be the major force in her life or whether she had a right to keep it in the background, maybe even completely under wraps.

Her phone rang a fourth time.

It could only be *him*—the man who had called the past two nights, the man with the compelling voice, tinged with authority, commanding in its intensity as it directed her to return his call. She didn't know what he wanted, but she could guess. Heaven knew how he'd gotten her number because no one in L.A. had it—not even the manager where she worked.

Her answering machine kicked on with her brief direction for the caller to leave a message. Her usually lilting tone was serious and cool. She ran her hand through her short-cropped light brown hair, ruffling her bangs away from her forehead. She wasn't used to the short cut yet. Her hair had hung in a braid down her back since she was a child. But she'd made changes since moving here—she actually had time to herself . . . to be out in the sun, ride a bike, take long walks. She'd found peace along with the bright California sun and she wasn't ready to let go of either.

"Ms. Kellerhern. This is Adam Hobbs. Again," he added in a deep, almost censuring baritone. "In case you haven't received my earlier messages, I need to speak with you immediately about a matter of great urgency." He paused. "Ms. Kellerhern, I *must* speak with you. Please return my call." He gave his number slowly, hesitated a moment, then clicked off.

Jana stopped dusting. He hadn't said "please" in his other messages. This time there was a quiet desperation in his tone. She recognized the emotion because the people she'd helped in the past had all been desperate. Adam Hobbs didn't sound like a man who was accustomed to using the word "please," and the huskiness edging the word made her feel vulnerable and guilty, two of the burdens from which she'd tried to escape.

Now this man had brought them to the surface once more. She *wouldn't* return his call. She deserved unpressured time to think about the direction of her life, to have fun working at something she'd never imagined she'd enjoy. Adam Hobbs could find someone else to solve his problem, someone else with a gift that had begun to feel more like a curse.

Chapter One

Adam didn't want to be caught dead, let alone alive, inside a beauty salon. As he pulled open the glass door and stepped inside, feminine chatter, strange smells and the glimpse of a woman with her hair rolled in blue and purple curlers was enough to make him decide he'd rather face ten corporate mergers in one day than to plow into this women's domain. But he'd do anything to find his daughters.

Anything.

Adam's determination had pulled him out of the poverty of his childhood, earned him a scholarship to law school and pushed him to start his own law practice after only a year with a prestigious firm. He'd wanted to be his own boss, bill his own hours, set his own standards. His determination couldn't save his marriage, but by God, it would lead him to his daughters. After six months of dead ends, he'd decided money and rational strategies weren't enough. That's why he was here. That's why he had to speak to Jana Kellerhern.

At his P.I.'s insistence, Adam had agreed to go this route—the only route left as far as Adam was concerned or he wouldn't pursue it. He wouldn't debate about methods, not even weird ones at this point. He had to put his logic and wariness aside if he hoped to find his daughters before he lost more time with them.

The woman at the desk inside the door smiled as her gaze traveled from his dark brown hair, down his charcoal pin-striped suit and striped silk tie, to his black wing-tip shoes. She tilted her head and her lips curved up a bit more. "Can I help you?"

Suddenly Adam felt as if he were the center of attention. Two customers on chairs in the room beyond had craned their necks to avidly assess him along with the receptionist. His shirt collar felt tighter, and he resisted the urge to tug down his tie. "I'm looking for Jana Kellerhern."

"You want a manicure?" the redheaded, perfectly coiffed and made-up receptionist asked with a mischievous smile.

"No. My name is Adam Hobbs. I need to speak with her as soon as possible," he said in his best authoritarian tone. "Is she here?"

"Hold on a sec," the redhead answered, her smile flagging. Disappearing into the room beyond, she reappeared a few moments later. "She's with a client. She says she'll talk to you in five minutes."

Five minutes. What the heck was he supposed to do for five minutes? He spied several magazines in a basket in the corner beside two directors' chairs. "Fine. I'll wait."

Waiting wasn't something Adam did well. He flipped one glossy page after the other, vaguely aware this publication didn't advertise fast cars or Armani suits. Tuning in to the sound of feminine voices in the next room, he tried to pick out the one belonging to a woman who had helped police departments solve missing person cases. As he had many times in the past few days, he imagined what she might look like. Probably fuzzy, wild hair with a red scarf tied around her head.

He could feel the receptionist watching him as she pretended to study the schedule book. Finally a customer with bright crimson nails came from the room beyond and gingerly opened her purse at the desk.

"Jana can see you now," the deskkeeper informed him.

Jana Kellerhern's lack of response to his phone calls had irritated and frustrated Adam. He was accustomed to being in charge. But his reason for being here brushed all that aside.

Striding into the busy room, he took it in with one glance—the chairs, mirrors, blow dryers, three hairdressers chatting to their customers. But then his gaze fell on the small white wrought-iron desk in the far corner and the woman sitting behind it. Her face turned away from him, she slid a pack of acrylic nails to the side of the glass top and straightened her manicure paraphernalia. At his approach, her gaze met his, and he almost stopped short.

She didn't look like a psychic.

Her short-cropped wavy hair was more blond than brown. It wisped in front of her ears, curled above them and ended in a fringe on her neck. Her bangs wafted across her honey brows. But it was her huge brown eyes that almost immobilized him. They didn't appraise him physically, they looked into his soul. He didn't like the invasion.

Jana had wished her client a good day and unnecessarily organized her worktable, hoping Adam Hobbs had decided not to wait. When she turned her head and saw a tall man with resolve shouting from his furrowed dark brows, the set of his mouth *and* his slightly squared jaw, she realized it would take more than a few unanswered phone messages to deter this man.

Taking a slow breath and maintaining eye contact, she stood and slid her hands into the pockets of her white apron. Adam Hobbs wanted something from her, all right, and she couldn't give it. Not right now.

"Ms. Kellerhern."

It was more statement than question. She nodded.

"Could we talk for a few minutes?"

She gestured to her desk. "I'm working, Mr. Hobbs. I really don't have time—"

"You don't have a client at the moment," he countered, his blue eyes steady, his voice firm.

This man could be intimidating. But she was used to dealing with hard-nosed cops, jaded private investigators and a disbelieving public who wanted her help anyway. "No, I don't. But I am working. Now, if you'd like a manicure..." She almost had to smile at his expression of distaste, but then his next words made her heart beat faster.

"I want a few minutes with you. You're the last option I have."

"For what?" she asked, though she sensed what he needed.

"My two daughters. I need you to help me find them."

Jana glanced around the shop to make sure no one was listening. "Where did you get my name?"

"Does it matter?" As he asked, he slipped a photo from the inside pocket of his jacket.

His movement was quick, but Jana caught a view of a narrow waist, slim hips and a physique probably as taut as his demeanor and voice. When he offered her the photograph, her attention returned to the situation at hand and she took a step back.

The two young girls in the snapshot had their father's blue eyes and brown hair. She could tell that he loved them from the way the camera had caught Adam Hobbs's expression as he crouched down between them, one arm around each daughter. The pain in his eyes now attested to the fact.

He tried to hand Jana the photo, but she wouldn't take it. She knew what might happen if she did. She might see images and feel emotions she didn't want right now. Folding her hands in front of her, she said, "I'm no longer doing that type of work."

But it was difficult for her to tear her gaze from the picture. When she did, the sadness in Adam Hobbs's eyes was almost as difficult to ignore.

"Why?"

For some reason, she couldn't hedge or lie to this man. Checking again to be sure no one eavesdropped, Jana lowered her voice. "Since I was sixteen, Mr. Hobbs, my life hasn't been my own. I came to L.A. to escape the type of work you want me to do, to make decisions about my future." She stopped and tears pricked her eyes as she thought about the last few months before leaving Indiana. Regaining her composure, she swallowed and went on, "For almost ten years, I've helped others when they've asked. Now I need time and breathing room before I decide if and how I want to use my gift again.''

As she spoke, she could tell he listened. There was a spark of empathy in his eyes, but, of course, his need was more important. "Take this one case," he insisted. "I'll protect your privacy if that's what you're concerned about. Your help doesn't have to be public knowledge. I'm a lawyer. I know what safeguards we can take. No one else has to know you're here."

She steeled herself against the man's masculine appeal and turned away from the wonderful smiles of the children in the photo as well as the hurt still lingering in her heart. That hurt sprang up every time she remembered Brian Reston and the search for his son, the months she'd dreamed about a future for the three of them.

Despite the time that had passed, despite the miles between L.A. and Deep River, Indiana, she knew she wasn't ready for Adam Hobbs and his search . . . for any of it. The general public thought psychics could "know" anything they wanted, that they could answer any question, even their own personal ones. That just wasn't true. Jana had realized early on that she couldn't use her gift for her own benefit or to predict events. All she could do was tune into impressions and use them along with her intuition. Words, pictures and sounds sometimes popped into her head, but she never knew when that was going to happen. It hadn't happened since she'd left Indiana.

With the need for self-preservation being her overriding concern, she said, "If you found me, others will be able to. And I'm not only concerned about privacy. You make my help seem simple, as if all I have to do is close my eyes and give you the answers you want. The process is much more complicated than that. Try a private investigator, Mr. Hobbs. It will be best for both of us.''

''A private investigator gave me your name.''

She sighed and shook her head. ''Then he can find someone else who does my kind of work.''

''It's difficult to find a reputable psychic,'' Adam almost growled as his frustration became evident.

Worry stabbed Jana. ''Shh…'' All she needed was her co-workers knowing.

Adam lifted his hands in exasperation and in a loud whisper asked, ''Why is it so all-fired important for no one to know what you do?''

Anger bubbled up inside her because this man knew nothing about the hundreds of letters she received each year, the sleepless nights, the burden of parents and brothers and sisters and children depending on her to find someone they loved, or someone who was missing. What irritated her the most were those who wanted a plan for the future without formulating it themselves. ''If they knew what I was able to do, most women in this salon would want a reading. They'd line up for hours waiting with bated breath for me to tell them their future. And if I couldn't tell them anything, they'd say I'm a fraud. My gift creates a three-ring circus, Mr. Hobbs. *No thank you.*''

Harriet came in from the front desk. ''A walk-in for nails is waiting, Jana. How's your schedule?''

Jana accepted fate's offer of a neat, nonconfrontational way to end this encounter. ''Tell her to come in. I don't have another appointment until four. If it's all right with you, I'll take my supper break at five.''

''No problem.'' Harriet's interest in Adam was obvious as she gave him a wink and returned to the front room.

He faced Jana. "I'd like to continue our discussion."

"There's nothing more to say. I have to get back to work and I'm sure you do, too. Call your P.I. He'll find someone else."

The look the lawyer gave Jana was not resigned. If anything, it was more determined than ever. But he didn't argue. "I'll call my P.I. But I'll be talking to you again. Soon."

With a lift of his brow and a wave of his hand, he was gone.

Jana first felt relief, then a strange sense of loss. But she was used to feelings and images not clicking. Eventually they became part of a bigger picture, and then she'd understand. But there was no bigger picture where Adam Hobbs was concerned. There was no picture at all.

The instant Jana stepped outside of the Hair Happening, she saw him. He stood beside a gray Mercedes in the parking lot. She should have realized this man wouldn't give up so easily. Ducking back into the salon was an option. So was ignoring him as she walked to the enchilada and chili stand across the parking lot of the strip shopping center. But she had the feeling when she returned, he'd still be waiting, and not quite so patiently.

A group of teenagers on Rollerblades skated by, one of them holding a miniature schnauzer on a leash. She smiled at the sight, something she'd never see in Deep River. But her smile slipped as she spotted the lawyer walking toward her, and an excited little shiver zipped up her spine. At least six-two, lean and fit, with long legs that quickly covered the distance between them, he was the type of man who could attract a roomful of women without trying. It wasn't only his looks but his confidence, his dominating male presence.

When he stood before her, he asked, "Can I buy you supper?"

"If I hadn't mentioned my break, you would have waited till I quit for the day. Right?"

"Yes."

"Mr. Hobbs..."

"Adam. You have to eat supper, I have to eat supper. Is there any reason we shouldn't talk while we do?"

"You have an ulterior motive. This won't be much of a break for me."

"It's not an ulterior motive because you know what I want."

"Obviously I need to watch what I say with a lawyer," she murmured.

The corners of his mouth twitched up. "Is that a yes or no?"

"If I say no, you'll be back. Let's get this over with."

The curve of his lips turned into a frown, indicating he was uncomfortable with her frankness. Jana's gaze wanted to linger on those lips. They were full enough to be sensual, narrow enough to enhance the handsome aesthetics of his face. She could imagine one of his kisses—dominating, forceful, passion-filled.

The image startled her. She hadn't thought about kissing a man in over a year—since Brian had decided to reconcile with his ex-wife. She'd not only lost Brian but his son, too. At the time she'd thought her heart would break. But she'd buried herself in her work until she realized she no longer had a life outside of her work. Not eating, not sleeping, working twenty hours a day was a one-way road to disaster. Thank God she'd recognized her destructive direction in time.

"I don't know what you have in mind," she said, "but the chili and enchiladas are good at that stand over there."

Adam perused the truck-restaurant setup near an island with palm trees and benches. "I haven't had an enchilada in . . ." He shrugged. "Too long."

They walked side by side for a few moments, Adam slowing his stride to Jana's. The breeze ruffled his hair, making him look less formal and imposing. She thought he'd start making his case for her help, but he didn't.

His arm brushed hers, his suit coat rough against her skin. "Have you always done manicures for a living?"

She registered the texture of the material, the strength of his arm, and her heart jumped at the contact. Managing a smile, she responded, "Would you believe I have a degree in business?"

"Neither seems appropriate for a psychic."

Her smile faded. "And what does? Theater arts?"

He stopped and faced her. "Okay. I stuck my foot in it. I didn't mean to insult you. But all this is strange to me. I'm a logical man. I make decisions and judgments from facts. I've always thought psychics were frauds. But my private investigator told me about crimes you've solved, people you've found. Even if I don't believe in it or understand it, what you do works."

"I don't understand it, either," she said quietly.

Adam had been fascinated by the woman since he'd set his eyes on her. Looking at her now, her soft, feathery hair, those wonderful brown eyes, her slender curves wrapped in a pink culotte dress with a white collar and lapels, his muscles tightened and he felt pangs of arousal.

Crazy. That usually didn't happen simply from looking.

Her soft voice, her calm wonder, urged him to step closer, to find out more about her. "Tell me about it. Were you born with this ability?"

She shook her head and pointed to the supper truck. They began walking again. "I don't think I was born with it. If I was, I didn't know it until I was ten. I was sitting on a dock fishing and a storm came up. The thunder and lightning hit fast. The next thing I knew I was lying flat on the dock, the rain pouring down on me. My head hurt and I was shaking all over. Mom found me that way, took me home and put me to bed. We thought that was the end of it."

His P.I. had told Adam that Jana was from Indiana and had lived there all her life. She traveled often but had never moved from the town where she'd grown up. L.A. must be quite a change for her. "When did you realize something was different?"

"A few days later. Aunt Flora came to visit. When she hugged me, I saw this picture of her sitting at her kitchen table crying. I didn't understand it. Later, I overheard my aunt and my mother talking. My cousin had dropped out of high school and my aunt was terribly upset."

"And there was no way you could have known that."

"No."

"Did you tell your mom?"

"No. I was afraid of the pictures when they came and uncomfortable with the feelings. I kept it a secret until I was sixteen."

They reached the vending stand. Jana ordered chili and corn bread; Adam asked for an enchilada. She opened her purse, but he closed his hand over hers. Her skin was soft and warm and a jolt of desire more powerful than before stabbed him. "I've got it," he said, unable to keep the husky rasp from his voice.

Her gaze met his. The sparks of gold in the brown told him his touch affected her as much as hers affected him. She pulled away, and he let go.

Jana busied herself pulling napkins from the holder while Adam paid for and carried their plates to a bench. Picking up their sodas, she joined him. She'd no sooner settled on the bench with her soda by her shoe and the cup of chili with a wedge of corn bread perched on the edge in her hand when the schnauzer she'd seen earlier ran over to her and jumped up and down, finally landing with her paws on Jana's knees.

Jana laughed and held her dish a little higher, out of the dog's reach. "You might want supper, but I'm not sure you should have this."

One of the Rollerbladers came skating over, his helmet under his arm, a leash dangling from his hand. "Sorry if she's botherin' you. She begs from everybody."

The boy was about twelve. His spiked brown hair was matted down from his helmet, his snapping brown eyes sparkled with amusement. Jana asked him, "Can she have a bite?"

He grinned. "If you wanna give it to her."

Jana tried to tear off a piece of the corn bread, but it slid into the chili. Adam grabbed the dish and held it for her. Smiling her thanks, she took a small piece from the wedge and let the dog lick it from her hand. The schnauzer gulped it down and looked up at her for more. Laughing again, Jana scratched the pet behind her ears. "I should have known that little bit wouldn't be enough."

As she touched the dog and rubbed her rough coat, Jana felt her gaze pulled to the teenager again. He and the dog were connected by a strong bond of affection. A surge of energy made her fingers tingle and she automatically closed her eyes for a moment. A clear picture of a dark-haired woman on a porch came into focus. The woman was worried. Jana had the distinct impression she was the boy's mother.

Opening her eyes, Jana cast a wary look at Adam. He was watching her closely. Should she say something to the boy about his mother? If she did, Adam would know what had happened. Why had this vision come now? Since she'd left Indiana, she'd felt normal—no pictures, no knowledge she shouldn't have.

Jana looked at the boy, knowing she couldn't let the woman in her mind's eye suffer unnecessarily. "I think your dog wants a full-course meal."

"What time is it?" he asked with a nod at Jana's watch.

"Five-thirty."

"Jeez. I was supposed to be home an hour ago. Mom's gonna be..." He stopped with a shrug as if a boy his age shouldn't worry about adult authority. Snapping the leash on to the dog's collar, he gave it a gentle tug. "C'mon, Peanut. We'll get us both some supper." He smiled at Jana and skated over to his friends, who sat on the curb sipping sodas.

Adam handed Jana her plate. "What happened?"

"You saw what happened. I gave the dog a snack."

"When you touched the dog, you closed your eyes."

Damn, the man was observant. She wondered if he was a trial attorney. "The boy's mother was worried about him."

"You felt that?"

"I saw that. She was standing on the porch waiting for him."

"You got that from petting the dog?" Adam asked, astonished.

She'd heard his tone; she'd faced expressions like his, many times. "Mr. Hobbs..."

"Adam," he reminded.

Calling him by his first name seemed too familiar. She already knew she could be attracted to him. "This 'talent' I have isn't something I can turn off and on like a light switch. It's more unpredictable than the weather or earthquakes."

"You made him realize she was worried without saying it, without telling him you knew."

"That was easiest."

Adam finished his enchilada and took a swig of soda before he spoke again. "My ex-wife took my daughters out of the country six months ago. I can't find them, my P.I. can't find them. Will you take my case?"

Chapter Two

When Jana's gaze met Adam's, the emotional and physical tug she felt toward him was so strong that she had to fight to keep her body from leaning closer to his. A voice inside her screamed, *You deserve a life of your own.* Yet her heart whispered back, *He's hurting. If you can help him, you'll take away his pain.*

"I'll pay you. Whatever you ask," he added gruffly.

Sometimes Jana wished life were black-and-white, that her answer could depend merely on an economic need. She thought of the people she'd helped and those with whom she hadn't met success. It had nothing to do with their ability to pay.

So she answered, "I'm not interested in your money."

"That's what my P.I. told me you'd say, but I didn't believe him."

"Believe him." She took another bite of chili, although her appetite had disappeared as soon as she'd seen Adam Hobbs in the parking lot.

"What can I say to make you take this case? Just imagine, Jana, if you had daughters and they disappeared."

The sound of her name on his lips created a turmoil inside her that led her to straighten her shoulders and sit up stiffer on the bench. "You're trying to manipulate me, Mr. Hobbs. It won't work."

His blue eyes had swept over her many times since their encounter in the beauty salon, each time making her more aware she was a woman and he was a very sexy man. But this time as he appraised her, she felt his respect. "The lawyer in me doesn't sleep," he muttered.

Empty plate and paper cup in hand, he stood and dumped them into a nearby trash receptacle. Returning to the bench, he shrugged off his suit jacket and flipped it over his arm. "Will you at least think about taking my case?"

His white shirt enhanced his tan and seemed to make him look even taller, his shoulders broader. She suspected he was a proud man, not accustomed to making a request more than once. Rising to her feet, she dropped the remains of her supper into the trash bin, then turned to face him. "I'll think about it. That's all I can promise."

The creases on Adam's brows relaxed slightly as he pulled a business card and a sheet of paper from his shirt pocket. "My office number is there as well as my home phone. Call me anytime. I go to bed late and get up early."

The warmth blossoming inside her at the idea of seeing Adam either late at night or early in the morning had nothing to do with the evening sun beating on her back.

He continued, "On the notepaper you'll find three names for references. The first is the P.I. who gave me

your name. You can discuss all of this freely with him.
The second name has been a close friend since college.
Jon knows I was thinking about contacting you to help
with the search. He doesn't know you're a psychic. The
third is the girls' pediatrician. I told her someone might
be calling to make character inquiries.''

When Jana went to take the card and paper from his
hand, his fingers folded around hers. "Thank you," he
murmured.

"Mr. Hobbs—"

"Adam," he reminded a third time, gazing at her with
such intensity, she repeated his name slowly after him.

Silver sparks glimmered in his eyes as she stood immobile before him, unable to tear away. She managed to
say, "There's nothing to thank me for."

Still holding her hand, fueling the warmth in her body
with his gentle touch and voice, he said, "Yes, there is.
For the first time in months, I have hope."

Suddenly giving Adam hope was more important than
her new life and demands on her time. Yet caution advised her to take a deep breath and step away. Pulling
back her hand, she broke eye contact and fingered his
business card. After a good night's sleep, maybe she
could make a decision that was right for both of them.

The cool morning breeze wafted in the window as
Jana stared into her second cup of coffee at seven the
next morning. A good night's sleep had been a sheer
figment of her imagination. After the three phone calls
to Adam's references, she'd heard their words over and
over.

Shane Walker, the P.I., had told her, "Adam Hobbs
is a top-rate corporate lawyer in this community. He

cares about his daughters and he needs them. The longer this takes, the harder they will be to find. I know."

Jana knew that, too.

Jon Wescott, the second name on Adam's list, had verified the fact that he'd been a friend of Adam's since college. "You won't find a better friend than Adam. He's helped me through some rough times."

Jana had left a message on the pediatrician's service explaining there was no emergency. An hour later, the doctor had called back. "Adam cares about his daughters a great deal. Since his divorce, he calls me every time they have a checkup or a problem to get the full details and to carry out my instructions."

So, unable to sleep, Jana had tossed, turned, paced, listened to music and finally cleaned out her closet until the sun rose, all the while seeing Adam Hobbs's face in her mind's eye. She couldn't forget him, she couldn't ignore him, she couldn't decide what to do about him.

Carrying her coffee mug to the bright yellow kitchen counter, she set it next to a Rolodex. Adam's business card lay on the counter beside it. She flipped through the file, pausing at one number, then another. It would be simple, really, to recommend another psychic. She wasn't the only one who did this type of work.

Her flipping stopped when she came to Brian Reston's name and address. She'd never taken it out. *Hanging on to lost dreams?* her heart asked.

Possibly. Or maybe she'd kept the card as a reminder of what could happen when she became too involved.

Was there a chance she would become too involved with Adam? His intelligence, intensity and physical impact were lethal. She could tell he was a man to be reckoned with, simply by listening to his messages on her machine. In person she'd felt the full power of his personality.

The scenario seemed too familiar—a man she was attracted to, an ex-wife in the background and children. She remembered the photo of his children, his voice when he spoke of them. The situation could be different this time. She wouldn't fall in love. Maybe this could be handled quickly. She'd help him find his little girls and return to the serenity she'd found before he'd called. No one in Los Angeles had to know what she was doing.

With a prayer for the courage and insight to use her gift the best way possible, she dialed his home number. An hour later, she climbed flagstone steps leading to his house in the hills. Like Adam, the structure wasn't pretentious but spoke of quality from the clean lines of the stucco exterior to the red-tiled roof. Stepping under the overhang, she rang the doorbell.

Adam came to the door in a white oxford shirt and dress slacks. She supposed he'd been dressed and ready to go to his office when she called. But he looked much more casual than yesterday with his shirtsleeves rolled to his elbows, no tie and the top two buttons of his shirt open. Dark hair swirled in the gap.

Her heart raced and then almost stopped as he surveyed her white shorts and red boat-neck pullover. A moment later, he opened the screen door and stood to the side so she could enter. She couldn't think of one appropriate thing to say.

As she slipped by him, she finally murmured, "Your directions were good. I had no problems finding your home."

He led her into the spacious living room. Spruce green and earth tones created an atmosphere of serenity from the extra-long sofa to the ceramic lamps. Multigrained oak glass-topped tables reflected the light pouring in sliding glass doors.

They stood and stared at each other for a moment. Finally Adam raked his fingers through his hair and asked, "What do we do first?"

"Can I see the photo of your girls again?" She could hope this would be simple, but she knew from experience, it usually wasn't.

"I can give you ten photos."

"Just one will do for now," she said softly and calmly. She suspected Adam was a man of action who believed forging ahead was the only solution.

Adam quickly extracted his wallet from his pocket and slid the picture from its interior. She'd been so afraid to make a connection with it the first time she'd seen it, that she hadn't examined it carefully. The edges were worn, as if he pulled it out of his wallet often to look at it. He missed his daughters. She could feel it as strongly as she could feel Adam's sense of loneliness in this house without them.

Taking the photograph from his hand, she sank onto the sofa and studied it. He paced to the windows, looked out, then turned around. She could feel his gaze on her. With her eyes closed, she held on to the picture and tried to let the energy flow freely. But after a few moments, she knew it wasn't flowing. She didn't feel anything. Except Adam's desperation as he waited for a response from her.

She stood and approached him, not knowing why she needed to be close instead of across the room. "Adam, what do you expect from me?"

"To tell me where my daughters are."

"You expect a city, a country, an address?"

He threw his hands in the air. "I don't know what the hell to expect. I don't know how you do what you do."

She had the strongest urge to reach out and soothe his troubled brow. Fighting the sensation, telling herself she would not get personally involved, she stepped back. "This could take time."

"How much time?"

"Days. Possibly weeks."

"But when you saw that boy's mother . . ."

"I saw a worried woman on a porch. I didn't know who she was or where she was."

He shook his head. "I don't understand."

"I know. But you're going to have to be patient and not expect a miracle."

"What you're telling me is we might not discover anything."

"That's a possibility," she admitted.

"All right. Fine. The picture doesn't do it. What next?"

"I think I'm asking for patience from someone who doesn't know the meaning of the word," she murmured more to herself than to him.

He grasped her arm. "I've missed half a year of my daughters' lives. How can you expect me to be patient?"

His grip was firm and commanding, communicating the same frustration as his voice. The warmth of his fingers, his body so close to hers, made her stomach flutter. Trying to ignore it, she pulled out of his grasp. "I'm not a computer. You can't feed information in and expect a printout a few minutes later. Pressure won't work, and neither will intimidation."

He sighed and rubbed his hand over his face. "I'm sorry."

Just as he wasn't used to being patient, she didn't think he was accustomed to making apologies. "Adam, I want to find your daughters for you. I'll do everything I can."

"And you won't let me run roughshod over you in the process."

She smiled. "Not if I can help it."

Some of the tension between them dissipated. But the silver sparks in his eyes warned her again not to get too close. "Show me where your girls spent the most time."

Adam preceded her up the staircase, leading her down the hall. He stopped at a closed door, paused, then turned the knob. Jana followed him inside, not knowing what to expect. A purely "little girl" room surrounded her. Peppermint pink and white eyelet spreads covered the two beds. One was a youth bed with side rails, the other was a regular single. The white walls were smattered with pictures of puppies and kittens, a tiger cub and a baby seal. A white wicker desk bore the same scroll design as the headboards.

But what surprised Jana the most was the disorder of the room. A pink cotton nightgown hung haphazardly on the corner of one bed and stuffed toys were sprawled across both. At least three pairs of sneakers strayed across the pale pink carpeting. Several dolls, doll clothes and a miniature cradle lay in the section of the room with two bedroom chairs and a small table littered with crayons and markers. Jana also noticed the baseball glove, cap and plastic ball tossed haphazardly into a corner.

"This is the way they left it the last time they stayed with me."

The pain in his voice wrenched Jana's heart. "How often did they come over?"

"Usually every other weekend. A few days over Christmas vacation. A week here and there in the summer." He crossed to the bedside table and picked up a photograph.

Jana peered around his shoulders. His daughters were in the photograph, but so was a beautiful raven-haired woman wearing a large picture hat. It was tilted back and didn't hide any of the contours of her face. "Is that your ex-wife?" The question had popped out before she could catch it.

"Yes." With a last look at the photograph, he set it on the nightstand.

Restrained emotion etched Adam's forehead and a slew of questions ran through Jana's mind. Did he still love his ex-wife? How long had they been married? Did he have regrets?

She had no right to ask those questions. But others might help her get her bearings. "What are your daughters' names?"

"Karla and Stacey." He moved to a set of louvered doors and opened them. Half of the long closet was filled with children's toys and games, the other half held an assortment of girls' outfits and shoes. "What do you need?"

She was beginning to believe what she needed was more than a few miles between her and Adam Hobbs. But she'd agreed to help him and she would. The problem was he was distracting her. Every one of her senses came alive when he got within a foot. All he had to do was look at her and she felt an inner trembling. She couldn't work with her receptors blocked.

"Do you trust me?"

His blue eyes narrowed. "I'm not sure I trust anyone anymore. Why?"

"Because I'd like to spend some time here alone."

"You want me to leave."

She understood that leaving this room was as difficult for him as entering it. Unable to stop herself, she put her hand on his arm. "Adam, I feel your pain. I need to make a connection with the girls, not with you."

He searched her face for a long moment. She thought he leaned closer, but that must have been her imagination. Yet she didn't imagine his finger lifting her chin or the silver in his blue eyes as he bent his head. She thought of Brian, her need to stay detached, the look in Adam's eyes as he'd studied the picture of his daughters and ex-wife. And before something they'd both regret could happen, she stepped away.

Picking up a teddy bear on the bed, she clutched it in front of her. "I promise I won't steal the TV or the family jewels."

A stunned expression marked Adam's face, as if he couldn't believe what had almost happened. His chest rose and fell. "There are no family jewels." After an awkward pause, he asked, "How long do you think you'll need?"

"I don't know. Why don't you go to work and keep busy. I'll stay as long as I need to and call you tonight."

"Call me the minute you come up with anything. If I'm not at the office, I have a service. I'll get back to you."

She nodded and sank onto the bed with the bear. After an uneasy goodbye, Adam left. Jana hugged the bear to her and prayed she'd have some quick answers.

Eight hours later, Adam drove home and saw Jana's car still in his driveway. What did that mean? She hadn't called him, but she was still here. Success or failure?

He experienced a visceral reaction to her that he'd never felt with another woman. He'd almost kissed her. Why? She wasn't anything like the lean, long-legged women he sometimes dated. But her big brown eyes, her wispy hair, her feminine curves affected him in a way that both disconcerted and aroused him. He couldn't seem to control her effect on him and that's what puzzled and miffed him at the same time.

Hurrying inside, he took a quick look around downstairs. No Jana. He climbed the stairs two at a time and stopped at the closed door of his daughters' room. Sometimes, when the worry and loss was almost overwhelming, he hated Leona. But then he remembered her flight was his fault. A spoiled only child, his ex-wife had always gotten everything she wanted...except her father's love and approval. Though outwardly beautiful and poised, that lack had made her deeply insecure.

The insecurity drove her to be the best mother she could be, but it also made Stacey and Karla her focus for life. Adam had threatened that focus. He swore. If only he could do the past five years over again.

Opening the bedroom door, he didn't know what to expect. What he saw urged him to either laugh or tear his hair out, he wasn't sure which. Jana sat on the floor with her legs curled under her at the low table in the sitting area, crayon in hand, as she colored a picture in Karla's coloring book. He knew it was Karla's because the coloring was confined to the lines.

Jana looked up when he came in, as if surprised to see him. "What time is it?"

He glanced at his watch. "Almost five-thirty."

She straightened and rubbed the small of her back. "I guess that's why I'm getting stiff."

"Jana?"

She met his gaze. "Nothing, yet. I would have called you."

Disappointed, frustrated and unnerved because her soft voice was playing over his body as potently as a woman's touch when his daughters should be the only thing on his mind, he snapped, "So you decided coloring would help you pass the time until you could tell me that?"

She stood and wrapped her arms around herself. "Adam, I don't think this is going to work. Maybe you should find someone else."

"No." His vehement response surprised him as well as her.

Her arms slid to her sides as she raised her chin and squared her shoulders. "Something is blocking my concentration."

She was only reading him a page when a volume lay behind her words. "You can't unblock it?"

"You don't understand."

"Explain it to me."

"It's personal."

He stepped close to her, knowing he was playing with fire. "Tell me."

"Adam..."

He lightly clasped her shoulders and commanded again gently, "Tell me."

"I left Indiana to get away from my..."

"Gift," he supplied.

She gave a small shrug. "I've been in California for twelve weeks. At first I was exhausted. I ate, I slept, I learned how to do nails, and that was it. No feelings, no pictures, no tapping into someone else's energy. I began to feel like a normal person. I started liking my life here, its easiness and peacefulness."

"But at the shopping center, you saw the boy's mother."

"Yes. It was a surprise. Not altogether a welcome one."

"But it happened. You still have your gift."

Frowning, she bit her lower lip. Finally she said, "I know. But I think part of me is fighting it. I do my best when I'm open and relaxed, and I can't seem to get that way now."

"What happened today?"

"Nothing. That's the problem. I held your daughters' dresses. I sat in the midst of their toys. But nothing came. So I thought if I colored in Karla's coloring book maybe—"

Adam's heart almost stopped. "How do you know it's Karla's?"

"Because she's the four-year-old—"

"How do you know she's four?"

"You told me."

He shook his head. "I just showed you the picture. I didn't tell you their ages. I also didn't tell you which was which."

Jana closed her eyes for a moment, tried to forget the hold of Adam's hands on her shoulders and his close physical presence. But it was impossible. She was more aware of him than ever. Opening her eyes, she stared straight into his. "I don't know if this is going to work."

"I think it already has. Sitting here today, you must have gotten a sense of Karla."

His fingers slid back and forth across her shoulder in what he meant to be a comforting gesture, she supposed. It didn't feel comforting. His touch seemed to link up with energy in her solar plexus that went absolutely haywire. "I might have guessed their ages from their clothes."

"Is that what you think?"

"I don't know for sure. But I do know you can't be breathing down my neck through all of this. Your scrutiny won't help, it will only hinder."

"Stay here tonight."

Her stomach flip-flopped. "What?"

"Stay in the house with me, eat dinner, sleep in Karla's bed."

"But I don't *know* you."

His thumb slid across her bare neck, creating a riot of shivers. "I think you know what matters. I need to find my daughters. I won't harm you."

There was more than one type of harm. "Adam, I can come back early tomorrow morning—"

"Tell me you don't think staying here will help."

She knew better than he did that she could tune into the girls' energy more easily surrounded by their possessions. "I can't."

"The bedroom door locks, Jana. If you don't trust that, you can ask a friend to stay the night if you feel we need a chaperon."

As attracted as she was to Adam, as powerful as the vibrations were between them, she trusted him. It was gut instinct. She didn't want more people than necessary knowing what she was doing. "I'd rather we keep this between the two of us."

"You're sure?"

Adam didn't realize how a situation like this could snowball. She did. "We don't need a chaperon."

His blue eyes darkened, his head lowered almost imperceptibly, but enough that his face was slightly closer to hers. He paused for a moment, then he raised his head. They both knew if he kissed her, she wouldn't stay the night and she might not return at all.

He lifted his hands from her shoulders. "Why don't I drive you to your place and you can get your toothbrush and whatever else you might need. We can stop for something to eat on the way back or pick up pizza or Chinese."

"All right. Maybe during the drive you can tell me what happened with your ex-wife and why she disappeared. That information could help me."

Jana could feel Adam distance himself from her, but she didn't understand why. Was he worried that if she knew his story, she wouldn't want to help him? There was something she needed to know before she got involved any deeper. "Should the police be called in on this or are they already involved?"

"No police. I know how the system works, the domestic courts, judges with rulings as creative as the lawyers who fight for them. It's a crap shoot. And I don't want to file charges against Leona so she's facing a felony. I know her. The more I give her to fear, the harder she will be to find. I want to see my daughters again, not jeopardize the rest of my years with them." He strode to the door. "Give me five minutes to change and I'll meet you downstairs."

As Adam left the room, Jana studied the open door. This man packed a powerful punch. Staying the night might be a very unwise decision.

Adam stopped at the foot of the stairs, Jana's duffel bag and hanger with her outfit for work the next day in his hand. "I'll take these up to the girls' room. Why don't you take the food out onto the patio?"

Jana went through the living room and unlocked the sliding glass doors, wondering what lay beyond. She hadn't explored earlier in the day but had stayed in the girls' room, hoping to learn something important. But she hadn't.

Balancing the bag with the Chinese food in one arm, she opened the door and stepped outside. The sun, low on the horizon, glanced off the cover of a rectangular-shape pool. Tables and chairs sat along the flagstone border. A wooden fence with a hefty latch surrounded the pool area. To the right, a jungle gym and swing set in primary colors led to the edge of the property bordered by sycamores and alders.

Jana unlatched the gate and went to a table by the pool. She'd hoped to get more personal information from Adam as they drove to her apartment, but he'd kept the conversation focused on Stacey and Karla. She sensed he didn't want to tell her about his relationship with Leona. Why? Because he was still in love with his ex-wife and didn't want to show he was vulnerable?

Jana had missed all the signs with Brian. She'd been too close to the situation with him to see, hear or feel clearly. The product of a bitter divorce herself, she had encouraged Brian's friendship with his ex-wife for the sake of their son. But that friendship had developed into a rekindling of old fires and a reconciliation.

After taking the cartons of food from the bag, Jana went to the kitchen in search of silverware. Adam found her there.

He smiled when he saw the utensils. "I have chopsticks if you'd rather use them."

"Forks are fine."

"Iced tea or soda?" he asked, crossing to the refrigerator.

"Water, please." She'd prefer to keep her body clear of caffeine or sugar. As he pulled out a pitcher, she asked, "The girls love the pool, don't they?"

He looked startled for a moment. "Yes. They're like fish. They've never had any fear of the water. Leona took Karla for lessons when she was a toddler. She took Stacey when she was a year old. At two she was becoming a handful. She'd just started sleeping in a single bed before..." He stopped.

Jana gave him a moment. "Adam, we need to talk about Leona."

The pitcher landed on the counter with a thud. "All right. What do you need to know?"

In his white polo shirt and black shorts, with his dark good looks and tan, Adam was the most attractive male she'd ever encountered. But she could feel a barrier around him that went along with the defensiveness in his tone. "How connected is she to Karla and Stacey?"

He turned his back and took glasses from the rich maple cupboard. "They're her life."

"So they're close?"

"Yes."

His one-word answer was sharp, and she wondered how much she could push. "Why did she take them?"

He swung around and faced her. "It doesn't matter why, what matters is that she did. They're not in any danger while they're with her, I'm sure of that. Her world revolves around them. And money's not a problem. Her father is bankrolling her and probably knows where she is, though he denies it."

Leona's father might be a possibility to explore. Although Jana wanted to pursue her line of questions, she was afraid Adam would clam up. Besides, she wasn't sure if she wanted to know about him and Leona for her own sake or to help find the girls. "Can you provide me with separate photographs of Stacey, Karla and Leona? I might be able to tune into one better than another."

After pouring iced tea into one of the glasses, he filled another from the water cooler next to the refrigerator. "Sure."

Hoping he wouldn't get defensive each time she asked for personal information, she explained, "Adam, I have to ask questions to find out if the information I'm feeling is correct, if I'm in the right time."

He set the glass of water on the counter. "I don't understand."

"When I feel something or see something, I can't always tell if it's in the past, the present or the future."

"But you'll tell me whatever does come up?"

"If it relates to the girls."

Pausing for a moment, he then asked, "What if it relates to me?"

He'd asked the question with an intensity she couldn't take lightly. "If I think you should know, I'll tell you."

His eyes probed hers. "You handle your gift very carefully, don't you?"

"I have to. For my own peace of mind."

He nodded as if he understood, but she wondered if anybody could.

After they'd eaten and Adam had given her a tour of the grounds as they walked off supper, Jana said goodnight and went to the girls' room to settle in. She laid a notebook and pen next to the one bed. Sometimes in the middle of the night, she'd have a vision that seemed like a dream. If she wrote it down, it often made sense in the morning.

Taking her toothbrush and a white cotton nightgown and robe from her duffel bag, she went into the girls' bathroom. The shower felt good as she tried to calm her body as well as her mind so she could be receptive to any energy she might receive. But she couldn't forget Adam's casual ease as they'd discussed the difference between California and Indiana, or his smile when she'd tried the chopsticks after all and ended up with more *lo mein* on her hand than in her mouth.

Trying to turn off the pictures, she blew her hair dry, deciding not to straighten the waves with the curling iron. Feeling tired but not particularly sleepy, she opened the bathroom door, intending to spend some time jotting down impressions as she settled in Karla's bed.

But when she saw Adam sitting in one of the chairs looking potently masculine against a background of pink and eyelet, any calmness she might have garnered vanished.

He stood and came toward her, his gaze settling on the scoop neckline of her gown and robe. Extending his hand toward her, he said in a husky voice, "Here are the pictures you asked for."

The message in his blue eyes was clear—he found her desirable. She didn't need psychic powers to read that. "Thank you," she murmured, ordinary words suddenly seeming hard to come by. "I'll work with them before I go to sleep."

"Jana?"

He stepped closer, and she held her breath.

Chapter Three

Everything seemed to happen in slow motion. All energy gathered into a cloud surrounding them. Jana raised her head, intending to tell Adam he was confusing her, that his presence caused turmoil within her that could be detrimental to finding his daughters. But she couldn't speak. The power of his blue eyes captured her words before they could become sound.

His hands rested lightly on her shoulders, but their imprint burned into her skin. She could feel heat emanating from him mixed with the colors of the rainbow that seemed to combine their auras in a radiant glow. His breathing was in unison with hers, both rhythms increasing as they gazed into each other's eyes. Reality became the two of them, close, wanting the same thing.

Adam took her face into his large hands and tipped up her chin until his lips were as close as the scent of his cologne, the warmth in his fingertips and the strength of his desire. She trembled before he touched her, and his arms surrounded her as if to protect her against the pleasure to come.

His lips were as mobile, as warm, as expert as she'd guessed they'd be. But his urgency and demand took her by surprise. He slipped his tongue into her mouth before the idea of protest could even form. And maybe that was his intention, to act before she could think about what they were doing... the consequences...

Thought vanished into sheer sensation as his tongue swept her mouth and need became a yearning chasm demanding to be filled. Trapped between them, her hands opened so her fingers could feel the taut muscles of his stomach. Adam groaned when she moved her fingertips and, tilting her head, he took greater possession of her mouth—exploring, stroking, arousing.

Nothing Jana had ever experienced had prepared her for this type of kiss, this type of need, this type of man. Her body tingled; the center of her ached.

Abruptly Adam broke off the kiss and dropped his hands. When she swayed, he caught her upper arms and steadied her. Her daze shattered into the reality of what had happened as she opened her eyes and saw the expression on his face. Their breathing was no longer in unison, though Adam's was as rough as hers.

The muscle in his jaw worked. "That won't happen again. I said I wouldn't harm you. I won't."

The kiss hadn't felt like harm. It had felt too... right. But if she told him that, she'd be stepping into the exact situation she didn't want. It would be better if they both drew a line and didn't cross it. She would have to make sure she stayed on her side, and she hoped he would stay on his.

Feeling something on her bare foot, she looked down. The photographs. She didn't know if she had dropped them or if Adam had.

He scooped them up and handed them to her without touching her. His gaze was shuttered, and he'd removed himself from the friendliness of supper and the passion they'd shared. Just as well. She needed to concentrate on finding Stacey and Karla.

"I'll probably be up and gone before you are in the morning," he said as if he were formally addressing a client. "I'll leave directions on how to activate the alarm system and lock up."

She nodded.

"Call me sometime tomorrow and we'll make plans for what to do next."

She nodded again.

He went to the door. "Lock it so you'll feel safe."

As Adam closed the door behind him, Jana didn't turn the lock. She wasn't in any physical danger from Adam Hobbs—she didn't need to lock her door, she needed to lock her heart.

The house was huge with marble and pillars. A second-floor balcony looked out over a winding driveway that made a circle in front of it. Stacey wiggled in and out of the bushes, playing hide-and-seek with Karla. The scent of roses permeated the area.

Jana awakened and sat up in bed. Fumbling for the bedside lamp, she flipped on the switch and automatically reached for her notebook and pen. As impressions came, she wrote fast and furious without stringing thoughts together. When she finished, she read what she'd written and without thinking once, let alone twice, grabbed her robe and ran down the hall, shrugging into it as she went.

She rapped sharply on the closed door. "Adam?"

No more than two seconds passed before the door opened. Adam stood there bare-chested, navy flannel jogging shorts hugging his hips. "What's wrong?"

His voice was husky with sleep, his hair mussed. The line of brown wavy hair that curled down the middle of his chest, dipping into the waistband of his shorts, abruptly reminded her this was the middle of the night. They were standing bare feet to bare feet with few clothes between them. Jana self-consciously held her robe together across her breasts.

"I . . . I probably should have waited until morning. But I managed to connect with the girls—"

He grabbed her hand and pulled her into his room. "Tell me."

She took a quick look around the wine and forest green draperies and spread, the rich mahogany bedroom suite. As he motioned her to the love seat in the sitting area, she brought her attention back to him. "Stacey loves music, doesn't she?" Jana asked as she sat. "She has a favorite music box she took with her, a wooden box with a kitten painted on the top."

He lowered himself beside her. "You saw that?"

Jana was too aware of the heat of his skin, his muscled shoulders, the worn flannel covering his lower body. Taking a slow breath, she said, "Impressions that came while I was dreaming. I'd studied the pictures before I fell asleep. But I . . . I think I was blocking the energy." She'd been too distracted by Adam's kiss, in too much turmoil to relax.

"And something happened?" he prompted.

"No. Nothing. But I fell asleep with Stacey's picture on my lap. I had this dream, but it wasn't really a dream because I've had them before. So I wrote down everything that came. The girls are fine. They're staying in a large house with pillars out front." Jana described the scene she'd envisioned with Stacey playing hide-and-seek with Karla.

Adam absently mowed his hand through his hair. "Leona's father owns property in so many places— England, France, Scotland, Australia. Shane checked the holdings he found out about, and Leona and the girls weren't at any of them. But they could be moving around or her father could easily have set up a dummy company and bought a few more properties. Did you get any idea of where this house could be?"

Staying with the impressions that had been so strong a few minutes before, she tried to sense the area, more concrete information. "No. I'm sorry, I didn't."

Adam was silent for a moment. "You said the girls are all right. What does that mean?"

"Stacey's happy, but she wonders where you are. She misses you."

He averted his eyes, staring at a spot above Jana's shoulder. "Damn, this must be confusing for them."

"Adam, I know how frustrating this is. I wish I could...do more. Faster."

He took her hand in his. "At least we have something. I'll see if Shane can get descriptions of Arthur Carrero's holdings. Maybe that will help."

"Arthur Carrero is Leona's father?"

"Yes."

The coldness of Adam's voice told her what he thought of the man. "You don't like him."

"I wasn't good enough for his daughter. I never had a chance to like him."

"Not good enough. You can't be serious!"

Adam's eyes darkened. "You don't know me, Jana."

She couldn't believe the hint of vulnerability she saw in his eyes. Maybe it was the dark shadows in the room. Maybe it was because she'd just given him news of his daughters. "I know what your friend Jon told me. I know how deeply you care about Stacey and Karla. Why wouldn't this man think you were good enough?"

Suddenly Adam realized how much Jana's opinion of him meant to him. He wasn't sure why. Perhaps he was beginning to understand that life had dealt her an unusual hand, and he admired her integrity in the use of her gift. He didn't want to see her respect for him lessen. He didn't want to see the disappointment in her eyes if he told her the truth—that he'd been a lousy father and the wrong kind of husband.

He saw respect in her eyes now. And something more. The same something he felt when he looked at her in her nightgown, robe and bare feet. Their kiss earlier had done more than aroused him. It had opened a part of him that had been closed, opened it just a tiny bit, but enough to make him want to shut it tight again to protect himself.

Leona had not only taken the girls. She'd taken away his ability to trust a woman.

"Adam?" Jana asked gently. "Why didn't he think you were good enough?"

"Because I came from a different background than Leona. Because I don't have blue blood running in my veins."

"You're a lawyer!"

Adam laughed wryly. "And proud of it. But he believes what I am today had everything to do with where I came from, and he's probably right."

"That doesn't make any sense."

Adam couldn't keep his hand by his side. He had to touch her. As he stroked her cheek, he said, "Unfortunately it does to Arthur and it does to me."

"But, Adam—"

Slowly he rubbed his thumb across her lips. "Shh. I think it's time you get back to bed." Because if she didn't, he'd soon be kissing her and persuading her to stay the night in *his* bed.

She looked hurt for a moment, as if she'd offered friendship and he'd refused it. Then she drew away from him and stood. "I'm sorry I interrupted your sleep."

"Don't be sorry. I want to know anything you discover about the girls—anytime, day or night."

She looked uncertain.

"I mean it, Jana. Nothing is more important. Not my clients, not my peace of mind, and certainly not my sleep. All right?"

"All right," she murmured and crossed over to his door. With a simple "Good night" she closed it quickly behind her.

He wanted to call her back, he wanted to kiss her, for a brief moment he wanted to experience again that breath of air when her kiss had opened his heart. But he couldn't. He wouldn't. He'd experienced enough pain for a lifetime. He might desire Jana, but that's all he'd ever let it be.

Desire.

Jana went back to the girls' room, trembling though she wasn't cold. It felt as if energy was trapped in her body, screaming to get out. Adam's touch, not to mention his kiss, created such a surge, she felt as if she'd ignite. Unless she could calm down and restore some sense of order, she couldn't trust what she sensed.

She paced around the room, lifted a coloring book from the table and plopped it back down. This kind of blockage and turmoil had never happened with Brian. She'd found *his* son within hours. But then Bobby hadn't been out of the country, just simply lost in the woods. And she hadn't felt this powerful attraction to Brian when she met him. Actually she hadn't felt this powerful an attraction even as they spoke of becoming engaged. Brian had been easy, friendly, laid-back. She'd loved the peacefulness she'd felt when she was around him—it counteracted her hectic life.

Peaceful wasn't a word she'd associate with Adam. Intense, overwhelming, sensual. Blast it! This line of thinking would never calm her down. Sinking into a bedroom chair, she rested her hands on its arms and took several deep breaths. Sometimes it helped to let her excess energy flow into inanimate objects—like the chair. Closing her eyes, she focused on the rhythm of her breathing.

After a few seconds, she shook her hands, then laid them on the arms of the chair again. Calmness was descending when Jana opened her eyes and stared at the nightstand next to the bed. She felt drawn toward it.

Sitting on the edge of the bed, she opened the drawer. As she shuffled through doll clothes, she found a small gold bracelet nestled in a corner. It was Karla's. Holding it loosely, she let the impressions come. Arthur Carrero's name flitted across Jana's mind. Karla was in touch with her grandfather on an ongoing basis. Jana could see a phone in the little girl's hand and knew her grandfather was on the other end.

Wanting more, hoping for more, Jana waited. But the impressions stopped. Should she go to Adam again?

No. The word was loud and clear, a warning and a conclusion.

Tomorrow would be soon enough to talk about it. Tomorrow Jana needed to hear the whole story from Adam about his relationship with his wife and his father-in-law whether he was reluctant to tell it or not.

Jana overslept. Not surprising since she'd been awake most of last night and the one before. She'd made it to work a few minutes late with her first appointment already waiting when she realized she'd have to wait until evening to talk to Adam. Yet the information she had was too important to keep.

On her lunch break, she phoned him. As soon as she gave her name, his secretary put her through. "Adam, we have to talk."

"You've seen something more?"

"I have a strong sense that your father-in-law has been communicating with Karla."

Adam swore. "How do you know?"

"It's just a feeling, Adam. I found a gold bracelet of hers..."

"Arthur gave that to her on her last birthday. Leona suggested it, hoping it would entice Karla to wear a dress now and then. But it didn't. Right now Karla's a tomboy through and through. Give her a baseball cap and a ball of any kind and she's happy." After a short pause, Adam swore again. "Damn the man. Arthur knows I've been searching high and low."

"Can we go see him? Maybe I can pick up something while I'm around him."

"He won't be pleasant, Jana."

"I don't need him to serve me tea, but a few moments in his surroundings might give us some clues."

"He spends most of his time at his office. Why don't I pick you up after work and we'll try to catch him there?"

"I have my car. I can meet you. Just give me the address." It would be better for her if Adam didn't gum up her vibrations before she met his ex-wife's father.

Jana met Adam at the entrance of a ten-story office building. He guided her inside and into an elevator, pushing the button for the tenth floor. Every once in a while he glanced at her. Finally she asked, "What?"

"Nothing."

"I know better than that. You're looking at me as if I'm some exotic species that escaped from the zoo. I've seen that look before."

"And you probably misread it then, too. You're an attractive woman, Jana. Men are going to look. It has nothing to do with your psychic abilities. Don't you ever tune into their intentions?"

"I don't use my abilities for personal benefit because I can't. And I can't read anybody's mind, at least not the way you mean. All I can do is tune in on impressions and follow hunches. At times words or sounds or pictures pop into my head. But my own thoughts and feelings sometimes create static that blocks all of it."

The elevator door slid open. Jana stepped out and waited for Adam. She didn't want to think too long or hard about his reasons for staring at her.

They passed a set of double wooden doors. Adam explained, "That's Arthur's home away from home. Lots of chrome and glass. He stays here when he works late."

Adam stopped at a glass door and turned the knob. A secretary looked up and from her smile, Jana knew she recognized Adam. "Hi, Lisa. Is he in?"

"Yes, he is. But I have to buzz him."

"Go ahead."

As Arthur Carrero's secretary informed him Adam was outside, Adam said to Jana, "The last time I was here I was madder than hell and pushed my way in."

Lisa nodded to Adam and Jana. "You can go in now."

Arthur Carrero sat behind a massive desk. He was a short man, balding, dressed in a custom-made suit. He didn't stand when they entered. "What do you want, Hobbs?"

"You know what I want. The same thing I wanted the last time I was here. Where are my daughters?"

Arthur Carrero closed the file folder on his desk. "This is an old song, Hobbs. I told you I don't know."

Adam's stance was as combative as his voice. "I don't believe you."

The older man nodded to Jana. "I see you brought reinforcements. Do you think a pretty young woman can get information you can't?"

"She's helping me search for them, Arthur. She has investigative tools my P.I. doesn't. I know you've been in contact with Stacey and Karla. It's time for this game to stop. If Leona doesn't bring them back, I'll file kidnapping charges."

Carrero picked up his letter opener, balancing it in his palm. "Just for argument's sake, let's say I do know where they are. My daughter has primary custody. This is not a case of kidnapping. She simply took them on an extended vacation. You're the lawyer, Hobbs. You know why Leona has primary custody. Chances are good a judge wouldn't let you file any charges.''

Jana's gaze was drawn to a faded photograph on the side wall. A house with pillars and a winding driveway. The words Château des Fleurs became as clear as a billboard in her mind. ''Mr. Carrero, your granddaughters miss their father. Doesn't that matter to you?''

''No, it does not. Hobbs knows why. Leona and the girls don't need him.''

''A child needs her father, Mr. Carrero,'' Jana said softly.

For a moment, Arthur Carrero didn't look quite as arrogant or as cold, and Jana held the hope he would tell them what they needed to know. But then the moment was gone. ''I can provide what they need.''

''That's guilt talking, Arthur, for all the times Leona needed you and *you* weren't there.''

Arthur Carrero stood. ''This meeting's over. Lisa will show you out.'' He pushed a button on his desk.

''For today,'' Adam returned calmly, though Jana could tell he was seething inside. ''Tell Leona what I said. She'd be the one facing charges, not you. Unless, of course, you conspired with her.''

Before Carrero could make a comeback and the bad feelings between the two men escalated, Jana placed her hand on Adam's arm. Lisa opened the door to the inner sanctum, and Jana gave him a small tug. His lips were still a tight slash, but his arm lost some of its rigidity. He led the way to the elevator.

Adam was silent until they stood outside the office building. ''I'm sorry you had to be involved in that.''

"Tell Shane Walker to check Mr. Carrero's properties in France, or those of people he knows. The Château des Fleurs."

Adam looked at her in amazement. "You got something?"

When Jana told him about the picture on the wall, he wrapped his arms around her in an exuberant hug. "All right! We're finally getting somewhere."

Adam's hug threw her into a tailspin. His big body surrounding hers made her feel fragile and safe, yet tingly and waiting in anticipation for more. But more of anything with Adam was too dangerous to contemplate.

Dropping his arms, he asked, "Would it be worthwhile for you to stay at the house again tonight?"

Worthwhile or not, it wasn't a good idea. Not if she wanted to keep her distance from Adam. Especially since they might already have the answer they need. "See what your P.I. comes up with. Then we'll decide what to do next."

He looked as if he wanted to say something but changed his mind. "I'll let you know what we find out. Maybe this will all be over soon."

She hoped so, for both their sakes.

Late Saturday afternoon, Jana was working on her last customer when Harriet stopped at her work station. "He's here again. Says he has to talk to you. I sure wish he'd stop in to talk to me." The receptionist's gaze was full of questions. More than once she'd tried to pump Jana for information about Adam.

"Tell Mr. Hobbs I'll be finished shortly." Jana didn't look up but continued her brush stroke on her client's nail.

"Whatever you say."

Jana wished the situation were that simple. She hadn't heard from Adam since he'd hugged her on Thursday. Since then, she'd tried to put him out of her mind without much success. Now, here he was. The thought made her heart flutter, and she chastised herself. Adam still had ties to his ex-wife. Not only his daughters. He didn't speak of Leona with hatred or bitterness. Only with sadness. Did that mean he still loved her?

Jana finished with her client, wished her a pleasant evening and tidied her worktable. Untying her apron, she hung it in the closet then went to the reception area. Adam was standing at the window, watching people walk by. His denim cutoffs and black T-shirt were quite different from the pressed and polished clothes she'd seen him wear before.

"Adam?"

He turned, and the hope that had glowed in his eyes on Thursday had vanished. "Go for a ride with me?" he asked.

She couldn't refuse him. "Sure. I'm finished for the day."

Deciding she'd rather leave her car at her apartment than in the parking lot at the shopping center, she asked Adam to pick her up there. When he did, she hopped into his Mercedes and closed the door. "Where are we going?"

"How about the beach? I need to sweep the cobwebs away. The ocean can do that."

"The beach is fine." Actually, anywhere with Adam would be fine. *Whoa, girl. That is not the kind of thinking you want to encourage.*

Jana sensed Adam had something to tell her, and she waited. He drove a few miles in silence before he said,

"Château des Fleurs belongs to a friend of Arthur's. From what Shane could discover from the housekeeper, Leona and the girls stayed there for the first month. But no one he talked with knows where they went from there. He hasn't been able to trace her charge card because she's apparently using cash."

"I'm sorry, Adam. The past, present and future converge. Usually there is no time in what I see."

"At least we know they were in France. Shane is going to concentrate his efforts there. The problem is that Leona and her father have the money to cover their tracks well. They can buy silence, hire a chauffeur so Leona doesn't have to apply for a license, hire a tutor to keep Karla out of school..." Adam smacked his fist on the steering wheel. "It's so damn frustrating!"

After a few more miles, he switched on the tape player. The music was a welcome substitute for the tense silence.

Adam had missed Jana the past two days. He'd told himself he was being irrational, but the house had seemed even emptier than before she'd stayed the night. Maybe because she'd been a diversion. His attraction for her had filled his head with thoughts other than those of his daughters and work. When he'd hugged her the other day, she'd turned him on instantly. Yet that hug had been a symbol of something more—a type of caring he hadn't experienced in a long time... if ever. Still, he wasn't ready to think about a relationship with a woman. He didn't know if he'd ever want one again.

Eventually he pulled into the driveway of a sprawling rancher. "This is Jon Wescott's house. When he's away on business, I keep my eye on the place. I often come out to this stretch of beach to walk and think."

Adam guided Jana to a path along the side of the house. He took her arm as they descended stone steps to the sand. Yanking off his sneakers, he left them on the bottom step. Jana set her sandals beside his sneakers.

As they walked across the sand, Jana said, "It might help me to know the whole story."

Adam jammed his hands into the pockets of his cut-offs.

"Why are you reluctant to tell me?" she asked softly, as the breeze blew a few strands of her hair along her cheek.

If he told Jana his story, if she knew he hadn't been available to his daughters, would she still try to find Karla and Stacey for him? With Jana, he wanted to hide his shortcomings and failures. But if she needed the whole story to zoom in on his daughters' location, he had to risk telling her.

He didn't answer her question, but kept walking, slowly, so she could keep up. "I told you Leona and I came from different backgrounds. I came from poverty, she came from wealth. I fell for her beauty and poise. I didn't see the insecurity underneath."

Jana didn't pry or ask more questions. She waited. They'd reached the wet sand when he added, "Arthur's approval meant everything to Leona. It did to me at first, too. My father had walked out on my mother and me when I was four. So I guess I saw Arthur Carrero as a father figure." Adam shook his head. "That was a mistake."

He stopped walking at an outcropping of boulders. Jana didn't seem to care about her khaki slacks and red blouse as she slid onto one of the boulders and waited for him to continue.

He wondered what she was thinking, what she'd think when he'd finished. "Leona wanted me to succeed to the same level as her father. I wanted that, too. Before the girls were born, she was as busy as I was with charities and foundations. After the girls were born, her mind-set changed. She wanted me home more. But by then, I was on the fast track. I wanted the same admiration and respect she gave her father. I wanted to provide her with all the material possessions she expected. And after Karla came and then Stacey, all I could think about was the poverty I'd experienced as a child. I wanted our daughters to have private schools, music and dance lessons, and of course eventually to step onto the campus of an Ivy League college. I thought the best way to prove my love was by providing as well as Arthur Carrero."

"What happened?" Jana asked softly.

Adam stared out at the ocean, remembering his disbelief and shock. "Stacey was almost a year old when Leona told me she wanted a divorce. I suggested counseling, but she said we no longer had any feelings to build on. The marriage was over."

Jana slid to the edge of the boulder. "She didn't want to fight for it?"

"Leona's not a fighter. She runs rather than face conflict. We never fought because she wouldn't. She'd either agree or just turn away. Our marriage disintegrated because neither of us faced our feelings and our needs, neither of us communicated them."

"Why did she take the girls?"

Looking beyond Jana to the horizon, he explained, "Because I was finally becoming a real father and that threatened Leona. When we were married, I left in the mornings before Stacey and Karla were up. I came home when it was time for them to go to bed. I tucked them in now and then, but I didn't *know* them. They adored their mother and I let Leona have primary custody because she was their anchor. Yet I realized if I couldn't save my marriage, I wanted to save my relationship with my daughters. So after the divorce, I used my visitation rights to build the father-daughter bonds I'd missed. Six months ago, I decided I wanted joint custody.''

"And Leona?"

"She saw me getting closer to the girls, when before she'd had them to herself. She wanted all their love, all their affection. I think she was afraid they couldn't love us both. I told her I was going to file for joint custody. Arthur must have pulled strings to get passports quickly, and she took Karla and Stacey before I could file, before their next visit." He paused, then said, "Arthur knows I'm bluffing about the kidnapping charges. There were no geographical restrictions on Leona's custody or my visitation. And I certainly don't want to see their mother convicted on a felony. What would that do to them?"

Jana slipped from the boulder and stood beside him. "You blame yourself for all of this."

"Of course I blame myself! When I was married, I didn't know how to be a father or a husband. And after the divorce..." He shook his head. "Knowing Leona, I should have suspected she'd panic when I mentioned joint custody. I should have reassured her that I wouldn't come between her and the girls. She's a good mother, Jana. She just wants to hold on too tightly."

Silence stretched between them, broken by the crashing of the waves, the call of a gull. Adam watched Jana's profile, the fluttering of her bangs, the straight line of her nose, the tilt of her chin. Her stillness unsettled him, and he had to know what she was thinking.

So he asked, "Now that you know my history, are you still willing to help me?"

Chapter Four

"Adam, you're human, like everyone else. Maybe you've made mistakes. So have I. But I believe you're a man of integrity who honestly loves his daughters. Why wouldn't I want to help you?"

He hadn't expected Jana's acceptance and compassion. No one had ever offered him that before—not so unconditionally, and he wasn't sure what to do with either. The breeze ruffled the sleeves of her blouse. The skin of her arms glowed golden in the evening sun. Suddenly he wanted to pull her into his arms, kiss her until the kissing burst into raw passion and all they wanted to do was join their bodies, not caring where they were, who they were, or what they had to face tomorrow.

But he was a rational man, not an impulsive one. He knew better than to act recklessly. If he touched her, he'd only want to touch her more. "Stay the night again tonight. You found success by being around Stacey and Karla's things."

She hesitated and finally said, "I'll need to go back to my apartment first."

The coil of worry and frustration Adam had experienced since Leona had taken his daughters released slightly, and he felt almost hopeful. "Pack your bathing suit this time. We can go for a swim tomorrow."

"I bought a suit to play in the waves, but, Adam, I don't swim."

"You never learned?"

She shook her head.

"Then maybe it's time you did."

"The waves are one thing, a pool full of water is another."

"Are you afraid of the water?"

She blushed. "I guess I am. I love sitting on the dock or watching the ocean, but when it comes to getting in, I'll leave that to the fish."

He laughed, and it felt so good. The last time he laughed... He couldn't remember when. He draped his arm around her shoulders in the safest, friendliest way he could muster without curving her into his arms to kiss her. "Pack your suit, anyway. You can always just stand in the shallow water to cool off. The weatherman is predicting higher than normal temperatures tomorrow."

Jana turned her face up to his, her huge brown eyes searching his face. His arm tightened around her and he almost pulled her into his body. Then he remembered what was at stake—his relationship with Stacey and Karla. He might want to take Jana to bed, but he wouldn't. He could control his urges, because urges led to entanglement. Right now that was the last thing he needed.

Yet, as he guided Jana back the way they'd come, he realized having his arm around her felt almost as good as kissing her. Almost.

Adam grilled steaks on the patio while Jana popped two potatoes into the microwave and tossed a salad, thinking about their talk on the beach and the way Adam had looked at her. She'd hoped he would kiss her, yet at the same time hoped he wouldn't.

Through dinner, the pull toward him didn't lessen. Afterward, as they sipped from tall glasses of iced beverages on the patio, Adam asked, "So what do you do when you're not solving missing-person cases? You said you have a degree in business."

Maybe it was the lawyer in Adam, but he listened well. He didn't forget anything she said. "When I got out of college, I didn't know exactly what I wanted to do. I'd helped several police departments over those years and they had referred me to others. So I wanted something with flexibility."

"For that, you need to be your own boss."

Jana took a sip of fruit juice, then nodded. "Exactly. So Mom retired from teaching and with some of her savings, we opened a craft store. We sell supplies, take crafts on consignment and teach how-to courses."

"What about your dad?"

"He and Mom divorced when I was seven. He took a job in Missouri. I see him about once a year. He never made the effort you made...you're making. I guess that's one of the reasons I decided to help you search. Because I can understand how Stacey and Karla probably feel with you missing from their lives."

"I've never met anyone as honest as you," Adam said softly as he searched her face.

She felt heat suffuse her cheeks. "You're exaggerating."

"I'm not. You're special, Jana."

"You mean my gift is special."

He leaned closer to her and traced the line of her cheek. "No. That isn't what I mean. Your gift is part of you, but it's not all of you."

His fingers burned against her skin. It was a heat that went much deeper than the moment. "I came to California to find out if I *am* more than my gift. But it's so integral to what I feel and think and see. Maybe I can never separate myself from it."

"Maybe you shouldn't try."

Adam's voice and touch tugged at her heart the way no other man's ever had. Fighting their pull was becoming more and more difficult.

Thankfully he leaned away, stood and took their dishes into the kitchen. When he returned, he held something in his hand. "I'd like you to look at this. Shane gave it to me." He put a map on the table and unfolded it.

As Adam pressed it open, Jana leaned forward. It was a map of France.

"I thought looking at it might give you a sense of where the girls are."

He always talked about the girls, not Leona. Did he think of her when he thought of Karla and Stacey? As Adam towered over Jana, his arm braced on the table, his expression intent, she realized she cared about how much he thought of his ex-wife. A warning bell went off in her head, and she bit her lower lip.

Focusing on the map, her finger went to a particular spot. "There."

Adam asked, "Have you ever been to France?"

She shook her head.

"Studied France?"

She shook her head again. "I took Latin."

He almost smiled. "The area you just pointed out is where the Château des Fleurs is located. I suppose Leona and the girls could still be in that area somewhere."

"I wish I could tell you more...."

As her voice trailed off, he picked up the map and folded it. "I'm pressuring you."

"You want answers. I'm sorry I can't give them."

He snapped the map on the counter. "We both need to relax. How about a swim?"

"I don't know..."

"It's a beautiful night."

"It's getting dark," she murmured.

"The pool has lights."

She didn't know why she was fighting the idea. *Sure, you do.* Her mind formed a picture of Adam in a bathing suit, and her insides quivered.

He waited for her answer.

What would they do if they didn't swim? "All right. I've never been in a pool at night. It'll be a new experience." She pushed her chair away from the table and stood. "I'll go change."

A few stars twinkled in the darkening sky as Adam lowered himself to the edge of the pool. He had suggested they swim, hoping he'd cool off. Standing close to Jana, sitting close to her without wanting to touch and kiss her was getting more and more difficult. The urge to pull her into his arms was strong. Too strong.

The sliding glass doors opened, and Jana stepped onto the patio. Even though a lacy white oversize shirt covered her from shoulders to knees, his body tightened as he glimpsed her curves molded by the white one-piece suit underneath. So much for cooling off.

With an uncertain smile, she asked, "How's the water?"

"The solar cover keeps it warm. It's just right."

She opened the gate and came into the pool area, unfastening one button and then another.

Adam slid into the water so Jana wouldn't see what was happening to his body. "So why didn't you ever learn to swim?"

After tossing her cover-up onto a chair, she came to the steps. "When I was little, I was out on the lake in a canoe with two older cousins. They started horsing around, and the canoe tipped over. The safety pillow I'd been sitting on fell out of reach. I went under a couple of times before my cousin Jim pulled me to a raft. After that, I sat on the edge of the dock. I didn't go in the water."

"You must have missed out on fun in the summers. Didn't your friends tease you?"

"Deep River isn't Los Angeles, Adam. When a group of us went to the pool, we gossiped and watched boys. We didn't care about the breaststroke or the crawl."

He cocked his head. "You watched boys, huh? The same way boys watch girls?"

"I'm not sure. Exactly how do boys watch girls?"

She'd turned that one around on him, all right. He grinned. "We checked out their smiles, of course. Who was friendly, and who wasn't."

"You expect me to believe that?" she teased.

He held up one hand. "Scout's honor."

"I don't think you'd want me to check with your former den leader."

As they stared at each other for a few moments, Adam realized it had been years since he'd bantered with a woman. Since his divorce, his life had consisted of work and his daughters, not much else. He'd dated a few women, women who were as serious-minded as he was. He'd even gone back to their condos. But the nights he'd found release for a physical need, he'd been dissatisfied, disappointed. He wasn't cut out to be a swinging bachelor of the nineties.

Yet, he hadn't been cut out for marriage, either.

Jana descended the steps, letting each part of her become accustomed to the sensation of the water. As it lapped up inch by inch, Adam gave in to the pleasure of the slow torture of watching her. His pulse pounded as she got wet.

The water at her waist, she raised her eyes to his. "This is deep enough."

He could see she was serious. The surge of desire that had aroused him gave way to the need to take away her fear. "Jana, water can be friendly. Would you like to learn to enjoy it?"

Her brown eyes widened. "You mean learn to swim?"

"It's never too late. You won't let me pay you for your help. Let me teach you." Before she could refuse, he added, "If you're going to be in L.A. any length of time, you should learn. You'll have more fun at the beach."

"Not if I forget surfing," she said in a dry tone.

He laughed and held out his hand. "Come on."

She looked at his hand, then she looked at him. "Come where? You mean I can't learn in three feet of water?"

"Let's try five."

"But I'm only five-five!"

"Trust me, Jana. I won't let anything happen to you."
He was sure of that, as sure as he was that Jana was different from any woman he'd ever met.

He could see the fear in her eyes as she walked toward him, but she kept coming. He nodded to the sliding board at the deep end. "You'll be sliding down that before you know it."

"Not in this lifetime."

He chuckled and backed up. "Just a little bit farther. After the five-foot mark it slopes fast to eight."

"Adam . . ."

"It's okay. You don't even have to get your face wet."

She lifted scared brown eyes to his. "You're not filling me with confidence."

He held out his hand again.

She took it.

Even in the water, or especially in the water, Adam could feel the electricity between them. Ignoring the messages it was sending to his body, he cleared his throat and said, "You're going to use me as a ballast. Let my hand take your weight as you move your legs as if you were pedaling a bicycle."

"And you believe this is going to work."

"Sure do." Holding out his other hand, she reluctantly placed hers in it. He could feel the rigidness and tension in her grip.

"I'm right here. Relax," he commanded gently.

"Easy for you to say."

Suppressing a smile, he suggested, "Pretend it's a beautiful sunny day and you're out for a ride through the park. You *do* have bicycles and parks in Indiana."

She glared at him.

"Close your eyes and imagine it."

She closed her eyes, her long lashes a brush of light brown against her skin. Golden. Even at night her hair, her face and especially her smile radiated a golden glow.

Cool it, Hobbs. You're seeing something that isn't there.

He didn't quite believe the rational voice that also denied intuition, feeling and a sixth sense.

Jana's body relaxed somewhat and she attempted to pedal. "Just keep pedaling. Feel the way the water holds up your body. As long as you keep your legs moving, you can stay near the top." He slowly worked his way into deeper water. "Now, I'm going to let go—just use your arms to push the water away in front of you. I'll be right here to catch you if it doesn't work."

"Let go?" Without thinking, she stopped the leg movements and began to go under.

Adam immediately grabbed her around the waist and held tight. "You're fine. Hold on to me."

Jana's arms linked around his neck and she held on as if her life were in danger. She might be in more danger in his arms than in the water. The press of her against him created a swirl of desire that almost made his arms weak. But they couldn't be weak because they were holding Jana. He wouldn't drop her; he wouldn't give her a reason not to trust him.

Her knee brushed him, and he sucked in a breath. Working his way through the water to the shallow end, he gently set her on the steps. She clung for a moment then took her arms from around his neck.

Adam hadn't let anything happen to her. Her own fear had made her sink. As he sat beside her, she scanned his long arms, his powerful legs. The sight of him in black, shiny trunks was plenty of incentive for her heart to triple its rhythm, let alone holding on to him as if he were a life preserver. When dressed, he was handsome. With next to nothing covering him, Adam's sex appeal was overwhelming.

Holding his hands was one thing, holding on to him when they could both feel every curve and plane beneath their suits was another. She was trembling and she wasn't sure it was from almost sinking under the water.

"Jana? Are you all right?"

She stared at his chest, the line of hair down the middle. "I'm fine. I just feel a little foolish."

"There's nothing to feel foolish about. Fear is very real. But so is the buoyancy of water. If you're in it long enough, you'll get comfortable. Give it some time."

Taking a deep breath, she stared up at the black velvet sky.

Following her gaze, he said, "When I was a kid, I wanted to be an astronaut. I guess I thought if I could fly past the stars, all my problems would go away."

The night all around them, the shimmering glow of the underwater lights, seemed to make sharing confidences possible. "The sky has always held a fascination for me," she confessed softly. "The clouds, the moon in all its phases, but especially the stars. As a child, I remember looking out my bedroom window and thinking if I could just reach up and grab a star, somehow capture the light and keep it with me, I'd understand why I was different from everyone else, why I saw pictures no one else saw. It was a silly thought, but it made sense at the time."

"And now?"

His voice drew her as the starlight once had. "Now, I know I'll never understand the stars, the moon, the universe, why I'm different."

"Not different. Special."

When she looked at Adam, fire leapt into his eyes and she caught her breath. The moment held too much intimacy for her to bear. In such a short time, he had come to mean too much.

She forced herself to remember his daughters, his ex-wife. Breaking eye contact, she wrapped her arms around herself. "I'm getting chilled. I think I'll go in."

He watched her hands on her arms. "Maybe we can try again tomorrow."

"Maybe. But you don't have to devote your time to me. If there are things you want to do—"

"Some work, but mostly I try to unwind on Sundays."

"I usually go to church."

He studied her then offered, "I can take you if you'd like."

"I don't know the churches in your area very well. It might be better if I stay here and see what I can pick up about the girls." Standing, she made her way up the steps and dried off with one of the towels on the table. "Thank you for the lesson."

He didn't follow her out of the water. "If you'd like a brandy or a snack before turning in—"

Quickly she shrugged into her cover-up. "No. I'm fine. I'll see you in the morning."

Adam nodded.

Jana let herself inside the sliding doors. When she glanced over her shoulder, she saw Adam swimming vigorously. His long strokes took him across the pool in no time. He turned and swam back. She was so tempted to stay and watch, to share a brandy. But this time she knew better than to give in to temptation.

While Adam showered the next morning, he thought of Jana. It was becoming a habit. The laps he'd swum last night hadn't helped a bit—the rush of desire he'd felt when she'd walked onto the patio had lingered even in his dreams. Damn, his heightened awareness of her was unsettling. And he didn't think it was all one-sided. Now and then, he'd catch a glimpse of the same desire he felt in her huge brown eyes. She'd turn away or change the subject, but it was there, mounting, growing stronger and stronger.

Toweling off, he wondered if she was up yet, if she felt uncomfortable being under the same roof with him when the attraction between them was so strong. He couldn't shake the picture of her standing at the edge of the pool, towel in hand, her suit wet, clinging to her. *You've been without a woman for too long,* he told himself. When he found Stacey and Karla, he'd forget Jana Kellerhern had even been in his house, let alone his pool.

He pulled on a worn green T-shirt and a pair of black shorts. Maybe it would help Jana to go through the stack of memorabilia he'd collected over the years—cards the girls had given him, drawings, Karla's reports from pre-school. While Jana did that, he could work on the Sheffield and Babbock merger.

Adam peeked in the door to the girls' room. No Jana. She wasn't anywhere on the first floor, either. He opened the door on to the patio and stepped outside. Seeing a flash of violet along the west line, he walked toward it.

He stopped when he saw exactly where Jana was sitting. If he'd had any doubt about her intuition before, it vanished completely as he walked toward her. She was sitting in the low V of a sycamore, facing the valley of rock formations behind his property.

"Jana?"

She twisted around, then stood in the tree, bracing herself on a branch. "I came out for a walk and felt . . . drawn here. Karla's very angry with you."

"Why?"

"Because you haven't come to see her."

Jana's words tightened his chest. "I wish she knew I was trying. Do you know what Leona's telling her?"

"No. Was Karla angry with you after the divorce?"

"Not that I know of. She and Stacey saw me more after Leona and I separated than before."

Jana stared above his head into the distance. "The feelings are strong. Too strong to be very old."

"But no place?"

She met his gaze. "No place."

As Jana stepped to the ground, Adam leaned against the tree trunk. "This was Karla's special spot. She came out here when she was unhappy, if Leona or I scolded her, when she wanted to get away from Stacey hanging on to her."

Jana brushed the bark from her hands. "You lived here with Leona and the girls?"

"Yes. Leona moved out when we separated. She bought a home in Beverly Hills. Arthur had set up a trust fund that kicked in when she was eighteen. Money will never be one of her concerns."

"But it was one of yours."

He felt invaded again. Jana could read him too well. Or was she using her gift? "Intuition or clairvoyance?"

She shrugged. "They're not much different."

To him they were. "I forgot. You said you can't read people's minds."

"I just got the sense that Leona's lack of dependence on you troubled you," Jana responded softly.

She was right on the mark. After a stretch of silence, he admitted, "I wouldn't let her use her money for us, for the girls. I wanted to provide. She agreed to live that way when we were engaged. Ultimately, my need to make us independent from Arthur is what broke up our marriage. Yet I couldn't have done it any other way."

As Jana passed no judgment on him, his mind slipped from old history to the present moment. Her violet blouse and shorts enhanced the fairness of her skin and the blond in her hair. She wore no makeup. Her hair was fluffy as if just washed, and he could vaguely smell a delicate shampoo.

The sun shining on the grass still sparkling with dew released the earthy smell of near summer. But all his senses focused on Jana. She was as immobile as he was, caught up in the energy zipping between them.

Breaking the spell, he asked, "Would you like bacon and eggs or pancakes for breakfast?"

A small sigh of either disappointment or relief escaped. "What about pancakes and bacon?"

"That's not a problem if you watch one or the other."

"I'll take the bacon. Flipping pancakes isn't my forte."

He pushed himself away from the tree trunk and tried to keep his thoughts on breakfast. "The girls and I always tried to break the record on how high we could flip them."

"Did you ever drop any?"

Remembering breakfasts with Karla and Stacey, he chuckled. "Often." By mutual consent he and Jana walked toward the pool. "Jana, I have a box of items the girls sent me, gifts they made and things they accomplished. Would you like to go through it?"

"It would probably be a good idea. But I'd like to do it by myself, if you don't mind."

He could feel the distance she was trying to put between them, but whether it was to maximize her psychic abilities or for personal reasons, he didn't know. "I have some paperwork to finish."

She glanced at him. "Mr. Walker said you were a corporate attorney."

"Yes. I've been working on a merger between two plastics companies for six months. I want to make sure everything is in order before we meet to sign the final papers."

"You like the work you do."

She'd read him correctly once more. "Most of the time. It's not as cut-and-dried as the public believes. This particular merger has been challenging."

When they reached the gate leading to the pool, Adam stopped. "Is there anything you're not telling me about the girls . . . or Leona? Anything you think I might not want to know?"

Jana looked more puzzled than offended. "No. Why do you ask?"

"Because you haven't mentioned Leona. You've picked up something from Stacey, Karla and Arthur. It seems a little strange you haven't mentioned her."

"There's nothing to mention. I'm telling you what I receive, when I receive it." His expression must have shown his frustration because she laid her hand on his arm. "I know this is difficult, Adam. But we've only been at it a few days."

A few days. It seemed impossible he hadn't known Jana longer than that. Because on some level, he felt closer to her than he'd ever felt to Leona. Life was strange.

* * *

Sitting on the patio, Jana opened the Father's Day card handmade by Stacey and Karla. Turning over the envelope, she read the postmark. Last year. Leona must have mailed the card for the girls. Had she been planning to spirit them away even then? Adam had said his desire for joint custody had spooked her. Was he right?

Thoughts of Leona, pictures of her, brought only static. Jana couldn't get a good sense of the woman. She could feel that Stacey was a vivacious, happy child; Karla emanated a more thoughtful nature. With Arthur Carrero, Jana had felt a distant coldness surrounding him. But Leona . . . Jana felt, sensed and saw nothing.

The glass doors behind her opened. She'd been sorting through the small carton of drawings, Stacey's handprint in finger paint, Karla's progress reports from preschool. As she sat up straighter in her chair, the pile of memorabilia on her lap tilted. Before she could anchor the stack, it toppled.

Adam reached the papers the same time Jana did. Their hands touched, and the energy she'd tried to ignore swirled around her until she was almost dizzy from its potency. She couldn't pull away this time and didn't want to. Adam's physical appeal, his nature, his love for his daughters called out to everything womanly inside her. She yearned to answer that call.

The remaining memorabilia fell from her lap as he drew her out of the chair and into his arms. "I'm tired of fighting this," he murmured. His lips caught hers and their eager passion was too tempting, too magnetic, too necessary to refuse. Their first kiss had been deep and intense. This one exploded into want and heat and demand that defied time and place and reason.

His tongue dashed between her lips, sweeping, stroking, searching for her response. Tightening his arms around her, he caressed her back in ever-widening circles. Jana linked her arms around his neck and slid her fingers into his hair.

He groaned, tore his mouth away and said, "Kiss me back."

Simply the words excited her. The hunger in his blue eyes before he bent his head again drove away everything but his scent, his texture and his need. His need became hers as she nibbled his lower lip and tentatively tasted him with her tongue. He drew her deeper, leading her into his desire, coaxing her to give as well as take. She brushed her tongue against his and when he shuddered, she did it again.

His hands lowered to her waist and cupped her bottom, drawing her even closer. His arousal was hard against her. Instinctively she moved, and his low growl made her tremble. Brian had never encouraged her to take the initiative. He'd never encouraged her to...

Brian. His reconciliation with his ex-wife. Loss. Heartache.

Jana tore away from Adam, gulping in a deep breath. She couldn't do this. She couldn't let this happen. Not again.

Gazing into Adam's still-hungry eyes, she said, "I can't stay tonight. I can't let this go any farther."

Chapter Five

Adam hadn't been thinking when he reached for Jana, he'd been feeling. Jana was the one who operated on intuition and visions; he was the realist who operated on facts and concrete information. He dealt with problems as they occurred, and this situation was no exception.

So he laid the facts on the table. "There's a strong attraction between us."

Her voice was soft, almost a whisper. "I know. I'm afraid it's keeping me from finding Stacey and Karla."

"That doesn't make sense."

"Maybe not to you. But it stirs up...energy...whatever...and I can't read signals that might be perfectly clear with someone else."

"Has this happened to you before?"

She hesitated. "An attraction has never kept me from doing my work or finding someone."

He turned away and rubbed the back of his neck. The urge to draw Jana into his arms again was so strong it was a physical ache. But he had to ignore it; he had to forget about his wants and needs and put the welfare of his daughters first. "What can we do so this...chemistry doesn't interfere?"

"Some distance might help."

Facing her, he asked, "As in miles? Maybe if I fly to New York, you'll be able to think straight?"

Her brown eyes showed her hurt, and Adam felt like a heel. "I'm sorry. But I'm not sure what you mean."

"It would be better if we're not in the house together." She gestured to the papers on the flagstone. "I can take those with me. I'm working twelve to nine tomorrow. I can come over in the morning while you're at work."

The idea of her leaving didn't sit well with him. When he thought about why, the reason was obvious. She could do her best work here, in the midst of Karla and Stacey's things. "There's an alternative. You stay the night, a few days...whatever it takes. I can sleep at Jon's house."

"Adam..."

"I drive over and stay now and then anyway. It makes Jon feel better about long business trips."

"You're sure you don't mind?"

"What I mind is not knowing where my daughters are. I'd sleep out on the beach if I thought it would help."

"Adam, there's no guarantee—"

"I know. But if we can increase the odds of information surfacing, that's what's important."

When he found his daughters, life would get back to normal. His attraction to Jana would be a fleeting memory. Stacey and Karla and his work were all he needed to make his life meaningful. His conclusion made sense, but it didn't quite ring true. He ignored the niggling doubt that he was leaving something out.

On Thursday afternoon, Jana was sitting in Adam's kitchen drinking a glass of water when she heard his front door open. She knew it was him. She hadn't seen him since Sunday, but his absence while she sat in Karla and Stacey's room hadn't helped. Nothing more had surfaced. This thing with Adam was a screen, keeping signals from coming through.

"I'm in here," she called, wondering what he was doing home in midafternoon.

When he entered the kitchen, his tie hung loose around his neck and he looked tired. "I thought I'd quit early today." He paused, then admitted, "The truth is I'm having trouble concentrating. I haven't heard from you. I didn't know if you were still coming over or had given up."

"I would have told you if I'd given up."

His gaze searched her face, looking for answers, looking for some sign of hope. "Let me shower and change and we'll talk. Okay?"

She had a feeling they were going to talk about more than the girls. "Okay."

"I'm having my secretary reroute important calls here until five-thirty. If the phone rings while I'm in the shower, will you get it?"

She nodded.

As she heard Adam climb the stairs, she suddenly wished the glass of water were something much stronger. That was strange. She didn't drink. Alcohol made her heart race. As she heard the floor overhead creak, she could imagine Adam stripping off his clothes. She took a gulp of water. A few moments later, she heard water running through the pipes. She could see his shoulders, his bare chest...

The telephone rang, startling her. She jumped up and snatched it off its cradle. "Hello?"

"This is Troy Johnson. Adam Hobbs's secretary gave me this number. I need to speak with him immediately."

"Uh...he's in the shower."

"I don't care if he's on the moon! I need to talk with him *now.*"

In her mind's eye, Jana could see a parking lot, an empty parking lot. A man in a janitor's uniform stood on a ladder by the marquis over the building. He was lifting down the marquis. S & B Plastics.

"Miss, are you there?"

"Yes, yes, I'm here. Hold on a minute."

She ran up the stairs and paused outside the door to Adam's room. It was open. Going inside, she heard sounds from the bathroom. She knocked softly on the door. It opened.

Adam had a towel wrapped around his hips, casually tucked at the waist. Lower than the waist. It covered more than his bathing suit, but his wet hair, the drops of water still dewed on his shoulders made her catch her breath.

"Jana?"

She pulled herself together. "The phone. Troy Johnson."

He looked puzzled. "I'll get it up here. Go ahead and hang up when you get downstairs."

A few minutes later, Adam hurried down the steps. Dressed in a crisp white oxford shirt and dress slacks, he asked Jana, "Will you stay until I get back? Or do you have to be at work?"

"I can stay. I had a short shift today. I work ten hours tomorrow."

He lifted his suit coat from the back of the sofa. "I don't know how long this will take. I hope it's a false alarm."

"Problems?"

"We'll see."

Adam's professional guard was in place. She imagined he'd be tough when negotiating. She had the distinct impression no amount of negotiating would close this merger. Should she tell him?

On his way to the door, Adam called back, "I'll pick up something for supper on my way back."

He left before she could put the intangible into words.

Jana was sitting in the girls' bedroom, paging through Karla's books when Adam returned. He came into the room, looking beat.

"Tough meeting?"

"Tough doesn't begin to describe it. The Sheffield-Babbock merger fell through. Sheffield backed out and won't say why. An hour and a half of grilling and cajoling didn't make him change his mind. I can't understand what happened."

"Neither can Babbock," she said as she felt it.

"Excuse me?" Adam was looking at her with a strange expression on his face.

"It's just something I sensed."

His blue eyes became suspicious. "Just when did you sense this?"

"Now."

"Why do I get the feeling there's more?"

"When Troy Johnson called, I could see someone taking down a sign for S & B Plastics."

"And you didn't tell me?"

"There was nothing to tell. I didn't know what it meant."

"It meant the companies were going to start doing business together next week and then for some unearthly reason that you might know, Sheffield changed his mind."

"I don't know."

"And I'm supposed to believe you?"

"Sometimes the pictures I see are vague and I interpret them incorrectly. That's why I didn't say anything."

Suspicions still lingered in Adam's narrowed eyes. He was looking at her as if he didn't know her, as if she'd done something terribly wrong.

"Adam—"

The phone interrupted. She waited to see if he'd let his answering machine take the call, but he said, "I'd better get it. It could have something to do with Sheffield."

He waited for a moment as if she could confirm or deny. She could do neither. When he left the room, she felt empty, alone. They weren't unusual feelings. Her gift often caused her to feel them.

Adam returned to the room, his face grim. His carefully controlled voice held an angry edge. "That was Shane. Leona and a French businessman named Jean Watteau were spotted at Orly a few days ago. Watteau flew to Hong Kong. There's no record of Leona taking a flight out. When Shane's contact tried to question Watteau, the man denied any knowledge of Leona Carrero." Adam paced across the room. "If we don't find them soon, she could move Stacey and Karla out of France."

"Can you put a tail on Watteau?"

"Sure. And follow him all over the globe. Dammit, Jana, why aren't we getting anywhere?"

"You mean why can't *I* get anywhere."

"Are you sure you're telling me everything you know?"

"I've told you everything that's come up about Stacey and Karla."

"The way you told me about the sign? How can I be sure?"

His doubts hurt, but nothing she could say would take them away. "You can't unless you trust me."

"I told you before, I don't trust anyone."

"Maybe that's the problem."

"No, the problem is putting my hopes in the likes of someone like you." He swore. "I must have been crazy expecting some kind of universal inspiration to intervene."

"You regret contacting me."

"Yes. Yes, I do."

She couldn't help him if he didn't want her help. And even if he did, she wasn't sure she could make a difference. "Then you'd better stick with Shane Walker. He works with the concrete. I don't. I'm sorry I couldn't help you, Adam. I certainly wanted to."

She took her purse from the top of the dresser and her duffel bag from beside it. "I'll show myself out. I hope you find your daughters, Adam. For their sake and yours."

When she passed him to go out the door, he didn't move a muscle. His blue eyes were as cold as ice. She was making the right decision. Now all she had to do was forget Adam Hobbs and Karla and Stacey. That was all.

Adam confirmed final arrangements with the caterer for Sunday evening and hung up the phone. He wasn't in the mood for a party, even though it was business oriented. But it had to be done. Pushing his chair away from his desk, Adam stood and stared out the window of his seventh-floor office. What should he do about Jana? His blowup had been a mistake and not altogether directed at her. Six months of work had gone down the drain. And then when she didn't tell him...what? That she'd seen someone taking down a sign? What good would that have done him except maybe prepared him for the session to come.

He glanced at the phone. Trust. It seemed to be a simple word. But it wasn't. His father's abandonment, his mother's death, had left him with no one to count on so he'd convinced himself he could rely on only himself. Then he'd met Leona...and Arthur.

Naively Adam had trusted Arthur to eventually accept him into the family. He never had. And maybe Adam had sensed Arthur's attitude in his daughter because Adam had never really shared his feelings and needs with Leona. He'd never told her how much he'd wanted Arthur's approval. He'd never told her about his fears, only about his ambition. But he'd guessed that was all she'd wanted to hear.

He had trusted Leona with their daughters. Look where that had gotten him. Wasn't that enough reason to think Jana might keep something from him? Except, why would she? Jana wasn't Leona. He and Jana were on the same side.

He might as well admit it—he still needed her. She wasn't a fraud simply because she couldn't give him what he wanted, when he wanted it. In fact, she was a strong woman who'd stood up to him in her quiet way. Leona had never done that. His ex-wife would sullenly withdraw when they had a disagreement. She never confronted him head-on. Jana didn't take any baloney.

There was only one thing to do. Invite her to a party.

Purposely Jana arrived at Adam's house a half hour later than he told her. She wanted to make sure she wasn't alone with him. From the number of cars parked in the driveway and along the edge of the property, she needn't have worried.

His call had been unexpected, even though her instincts had told her she and Adam weren't finished yet. He'd said he was throwing a party. Her first inclination had been to refuse. But the slight unsureness as he'd asked her made her realize they needed to talk one last time, even if she wasn't going to continue helping him.

He'd told her to dress casually. She hoped her sleeveless black jumpsuit qualified. When she rang the doorbell, a maid let her inside. Jana stood at the edge of the living room, trying to get her bearings.

At least twenty people milled around the living room and dining room. Jana could see others clustered on the patio. She didn't spot Adam anywhere. Crossing over to the bar set up in a corner, she asked for orange juice. The waiter supplied it with a smile.

Restless, not sure if she should stay, she went out on the patio. Two men in dress slacks and polo shirts stood by the pool. She overheard the gray-haired man say, "I heard Hobbs raked Sheffield over the coals."

The man standing beside him answered, "It didn't do any good. The old guy clammed up and simply said he wouldn't sign. But Adam won't give up. He never does. He'll get Babbock that merger one way or another."

"Do you think Carrero had anything to do with it?"

"I suppose it's possible. But why would he interfere?"

The gray-haired man answered, "He's never liked Adam. That's no secret."

"Because Adam wouldn't bend to Carrero's dictates. Decided to stay his own man. Good decision if you ask me."

"Yet, it could be coming back to haunt him now."

A hand on Jana's shoulder startled her. She turned quickly, almost spilling her juice, and found herself face-to-face with a handsome dark-haired man with appraising green eyes.

"Jana?"

She nodded, recognizing the voice.

"I'm Jon Wescott," he said as he extended his hand. "One of the guests corralled Adam to talk business, and he asked me to keep an eye out for you. I must have missed you when you came in."

Jon looked casually relaxed in khaki slacks and a tan camp shirt. He was almost as tall as Adam. She shook his hand. "It's nice to meet you. Adam speaks of you often."

"We go way back. Why don't we go inside and get something to eat?"

Jon led Jana to the kitchen where a waiter stood at the table, ready to help serve from the many selections of food.

"Adam certainly knows how to throw a party," Jana murmured.

Jon took a plate from the end of the counter. "He wanted to cancel it, but he knew he shouldn't. Contacts are too crucial in his profession."

Jana glanced around her. "I didn't expect so many people."

Jon waited for her to make her choices first, then made his. "I think he was concerned you wouldn't come."

She couldn't tell if Jon Wescott was fishing for information or just stating a fact. "You're Adam's closest friend, aren't you?"

"Did Adam tell you that?"

Jana didn't need Adam to tell her. It was a fact she'd known as soon as she'd talked to Jon Wescott on the phone. "It's something in his voice when he talks about you."

That explanation seemed to satisfy him. "Adam's a very solitary man. Especially over this situation with Stacey and Karla. He doesn't want anyone to see how deeply their disappearance has affected him."

Jana could feel how much it affected him. She suddenly had thousands of questions about Adam that Jon might be able to answer. But she knew she had to find out the answers herself. Instead of questions about Adam, she asked, "Do you know Leona?"

"Yes." The word stood by itself until Jon asked, "Are you making any progress finding Karla and Stacey?"

"Sometimes I think we are, other times I'm not sure."

Hairs prickled on the back of Jana's neck and all her senses alerted her that Adam was close by. Suddenly he was standing beside her and smiling at Jon. "Thanks."

Jon nodded. "It was a pleasure meeting you, Jana." He took a fork from the silverware holder. "Maybe we can talk again later."

She had a feeling Jon was looking out for Adam's interests. She couldn't fault him for that.

As Jon moved away, Adam's gaze caught hers. "Can we talk privately for a few minutes?"

The power of his blue eyes hadn't lessened nor had her attraction to him. "I'm not sure I should stay."

"That's why I wanted Jon to keep you company until I could get to you. Let's go to my office."

Placing her plate and glass on the counter, she followed him. She'd never entered Adam's office. It was located down a short hall from the dining room. After she stepped inside, he closed the door. Cases of bookshelves lined two walls. A computer sat at a station beside the mahogany desk.

Before she'd taken more than a quick glance around the room, he said, "I was wrong the other day. I still want you to help me find the girls."

"Adam, this search is getting harder instead of easier."

"That's not true. I know more now than before I contacted you." He approached her slowly. "When I came home early the other day, I was going to suggest that maybe we both need to lighten up. So what if we kiss now and then? So what if we give into natural urges? Maybe if we stop fighting the chemistry, whatever's blocking you will vanish."

His theory was interesting and oh, so tempting to try. "I don't think it's that easy. At least not for me."

He searched her face for what seemed a long time. "Jana, if you want me to stay away from you, I'll stay away. I think we're close to finding Stacey and Karla. You can only speed up the process."

A smile sang in her heart because she and Adam weren't finished. Not yet. "You're using your intuition?"

At her playful question, he relaxed. "Powers of deduction," he responded with a grin.

"There's nothing wrong with a man using intuition," she offered quietly.

His eyes held her in place as he stroked her cheek. "My intuition tells me it will be very difficult to stay away from you. Is that what you want?"

What she wanted wasn't the issue. "I need to concentrate on the girls, Adam. Not on feelings between us."

He frowned and dropped his hand. "Then let's concentrate on them."

Did she hear a "for now" in his voice? Exactly what would happened when and if they did find the girls?

"I'd like to tell Jon that you're a psychic."

"I don't know, Adam."

"I'd trust him with my life."

The confidence and sincerity in his voice were enough to convince her. "All right."

"But you need to know he's a newspaper publisher."

"Adam!"

"I'd still trust him with my life."

She shook her head. "I've talked to the man for a few minutes and you want me to trust him to keep my secret when it would sell his newspapers?"

Adam looked as if he wanted to touch her, but he kept his hands by his sides. "What does your intuition tell you?"

"To trust your friendship with him. But I'd like to talk with him a little longer and then decide."

Adam took her hand. "Then let's go find Jon."

He was forging ahead again. That shouldn't be a surprise anymore. This time she followed him, thinking maybe it was time she did some forging of her own.

Arthur Carrero didn't strike Jana as a man who liked surprises. So early Monday morning, she phoned Car-

rero's office and asked how soon she could see him. His
secretary informed Jana he had an eight-thirty slot open.
Jana snapped it up. She didn't have to be at work until
ten. She should have plenty of time.

Last night, she and Adam hadn't agreed on a strat-
egy, just that she would continue to help him. After
she'd met Jon, talked with him at length and seen how
much he cared for Adam and his daughters, even baby-
sitting now and then, she decided it was safe for Adam
to confide in him. Shortly after, Adam had been pulled
aside by former and prospective clients and friends.
She'd left before he could ask her to stay after the party
ended.

The more she thought about Karla and Stacey, the
more Jana decided she needed to concentrate on where
she'd received information easily. Carrero's office was
one of those places. Without Adam's presence, without
the enmity vibrating between the two men, she hoped she
could make some headway.

When Jana arrived at Arthur Carrero's office, the
secretary buzzed her boss. Shortly thereafter, he opened
the door to his office. "Ms. Kellerhern. Alone, today, I
see."

She stood. "Mr. Carrero. Good morning."

"You're not only much prettier than Hobbs, you're
more polite."

She didn't take the bait.

He gave her a wry smile. "Come in."

Walking to the other side of the room, he stepped behind his desk. "What can I do for you?"

"Maybe I can do something for you."

He looked skeptical.

"I don't think you know Adam Hobbs."

Carrero grunted. "I've known the man for five years. Ever since Leona informed me she was going to marry him."

"You would have preferred handpicking a husband for your daughter?"

"Not that it's any of your business, but, yes, I would have."

"And you had someone all picked out, didn't you?" Jana asked following her intuition.

Carrero's brows arched and he kept silent.

"You couldn't control Adam."

"I offered him a career with my corporation he could only dream about. He would have been internationally famous."

"But under your thumb. Adam's not that kind of man."

"You think you know so much about him, Miss Private Investigator. Maybe you should ask him why Leona divorced him. I might not have given Leona much time after her mother died, but I was a faithful husband while I was married."

Jana's chest tightened. "What are you saying?"

"Leona told me Hobbs had an affair. That's why she demanded a divorce. His secretary, she said. How tawdry."

Jana was stunned. She wanted to refute his statement, and everything inside her cried out that he had to be mistaken. But she didn't know for sure. Adam had been so reluctant to tell her about his past. Had he left this out on purpose? She wasn't sure which voice was crying *No*—her intuition or an emotional part of her that didn't want to believe Adam was capable of infidelity. There was only one way she'd know for sure. She had to ask him face-to-face.

Pulling herself together, pushing that question into the background, she said, "Mr. Carrero, I'm not here to delve into history. I'm here to tell you Adam loves his daughters dearly and has only their best interests at heart. He would never do anything to harm them. But your daughter is harming them by keeping them away from their father. Surely you can understand that Karla and Stacey must be confused by this separation. I'm sure you could see how much Leona missed her mother as she was growing up. Karla and Stacey know Adam is somewhere, yet Leona is keeping them away from him. Don't you think they'll eventually resent her for that?"

Arthur Carrero pushed his chair away and came around the front of the desk. "Why do you care, Ms. Kellerhern? What does this have to do with you? You're probably getting paid a day rate whether you find the girls or not."

He'd assumed she was a private investigator. It wouldn't hurt to let him keep thinking that. "I'm the product of a divorce. I know how much it hurt me. Adam cares about Karla and Stacey as much as Leona does, and it's criminal to keep him from them."

For the briefest instant, Carrero looked unsure. But then his guarded expression was back in place almost as quick as she could blink. "Time usually takes care of everything, Ms. Kellerhern."

"Time never heals loss. Karla and Stacey are losing precious time with Adam." At the unyielding set of his mouth, she asked, "Will you relate my concerns to your daughter?"

"*If* I were in touch with my daughter, I would express *my* concerns."

Seeing that Carrero wouldn't budge from his stance, Jana simply wanted to touch him. Gut instinct told her that was more important than standing in his office arguing with him. She extended her hand. "I won't take up any more of your time. Thank you for agreeing to see me."

He hesitated, then shook her hand. A word sounded in Jana's mind. *Gite*. What was that? A picture of a green-and-yellow sign formed with the phrase Gites de France. Quick on the picture's heels she heard the name *Dev...Devereau*. She waited, hoping to get something more. Something recognizable. Something she understood.

Carrero released her hand, and she knew she had to tell Adam what she'd seen and heard. Now.

Chapter Six

Jana telephoned Adam from a pay phone in the strip shopping center where she worked. She could hear the restrained excitement in his voice, the hope that maybe this time her intuition would take him to his daughters.

Then she waited.

The next morning, she was shampooing a customer's hair when Harriet approached her with a frown. "Your Mr. Hobbs is here again and he says he has to see you *now*."

Jana finished rinsing the shampoo from the customer's hair. "Mrs. Boyle is Marsha's client. Could you show her to Marsha's station?"

Harriet rolled her eyes. "I want to know what you two have going. Do you always go running when he calls?"

"This is business, Harriet."

"Yeah, sure. More likely funny business." She waved Jana to the reception area. "Go on. I'll take care of Mrs. Boyle."

GOOD NEWS! You can get
FIVE GIFTS — FREE!

If offer card is missing, write to:
Silhouette Reader Service, 3010 Walden Ave., P.O. Box 1867, Buffalo, NY 14269-1867.

NO POSTAGE
NECESSARY
IF MAILED
IN THE
UNITED STATES

BUSINESS REPLY MAIL
FIRST CLASS MAIL PERMIT NO. 717 BUFFALO, NY

POSTAGE WILL BE PAID BY ADDRESSEE

SILHOUETTE READER SERVICE
3010 WALDEN AVE
PO BOX 1867
BUFFALO NY 14240-9952

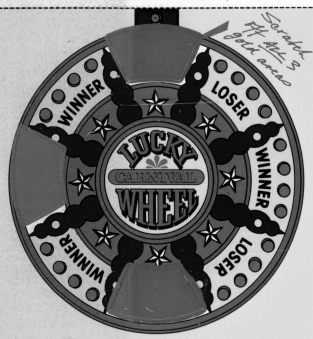

Harriet was a gossip and nosy, but she had a good heart. Jana smiled. "Thanks."

Adam paced across the empty waiting area as if he were a caged tiger. When he saw Jana, he broke into a wide grin. "Shane got it. *Gites de France* are rural cottages that are approved by the government. They range from small guest houses to medieval castles and are booked through the tourist office. Devereau is the head of the Loire Valley office. We have the address of the estate Leona rented."

"Oh, Adam, I'm so happy for you."

His arms went around her and he hugged her close. When she tipped up her head, his lips found hers. The kiss was spontaneous combustion. Heat permeated her body until she felt as if little fires danced inside her. Adam didn't seem to care that they were standing inside her place of employment because he broke away, then came back to her. Finally when she thought air was something she'd never need again, he took her face in his hands and ended the kiss. "Do you have a passport?"

She nodded. Two years ago, she'd traveled to England for a conference on psychic phenomenon. At that point, she'd still been searching for answers.

"Will you come with me to France?" Adam asked.

Oh, how she wanted to be with him, to experience his joy when he saw his daughters. But she had to wonder at the wisdom of making the trip with him. "Why?"

He looked away, then met her gaze once more. "Leona could move them again. I'd feel better if you're along to give some direction. I'm beginning to trust your intuition."

She'd proven herself to him, but she'd hoped he'd want her along for more than her psychic ability. "I don't know if I can get off work."

"Is there someone you can ask? I'd like to leave as soon as possible. We'll probably be gone a few days. Of course, I'll cover your expenses."

She'd have to let him pay for the airfare. But the rest she'd manage herself. The more ties she had to Adam, the harder it would be to get on with her life. Soon, she had to think about returning to Indiana. Except she wasn't any closer to a decision about her future now than she had been when she first came to L.A. Feeling Adam's hands on her face, she realized that decision had become much less important than this man.

"I'll talk to Harriet. She has another manicurist who works part-time. Maybe she can cover."

Reluctantly she pulled away from him. But he caught her hand. "Jana, thank you."

She suddenly realized that gratitude wasn't what she wanted from Adam. "When you've brought Karla and Stacey home, then you can thank me."

He ran his thumb over her knuckles. "I still can't believe you went to Arthur's office alone. He's an ornery old goat who thinks he rules the world. I found out today he got to Sheffield. Arthur told the man if he signed the papers for the merger, he'd never sell his plastics to foreign markets. Somehow I have to undo the harm he's done and convince Sheffield that Arthur's not all-powerful."

So the men she'd overheard at the party had been correct about Arthur Carrero trying to sabotage Adam. "Leona's father wasn't helpful, but he wasn't threatening, either. He's just a man who sits in his ivory tower thinking of ways he can get control." The accusation that Adam had been unfaithful resurfaced. She'd pushed it aside in her excitement of sharing the information she'd received and waiting for confirmation. But now she wanted her question answered.

Trying to ease into it, she said, "I think I know why Mr. Carrero—"

The phone rang. Harriet came in and answered it. Jana couldn't get into the question of Adam's fidelity now, rather she had to find out whether she could make the trip to France. And suddenly she knew even if it meant quitting her job, she'd fly with Adam wherever he went.

They left that afternoon. Jana knew Adam wanted to see his daughters as soon as he could. Their ultimate destination was the small town of Chinon in the Loire Valley. Jana had only left the borders of the United States once before, so the trip itself was exciting. But traveling with Adam, sitting beside him in first class and brushing elbows now and then, was even more exciting.

He seemed to take it all in stride, as if he did it often. His confidence and familiarity with traveling, including the process of going through customs, calmed her. With the calm came fatigue. After they left New York and the plane climbed to a cruising altitude, Jana reclined her seat and requested a pillow. She didn't need the black-out mask the stewardess offered. She fell asleep almost immediately.

A murmur of voices drifted into her dream. Adam was holding her, kissing her, touching her. She felt a hand on her hair, a gentle caress along the back of her neck, and knew reality from the dream. A blanket slid from her shoulders as she turned away from the window where she'd propped her pillow. She hadn't requested the cover and in her mind's eye saw Adam tucking it around her neck. Pushing the button to straighten her seat, she tried to blink the sleep from her eyes.

Adam smiled. "You looked cold all curled up in a ball."

"Thank you for noticing." The morning light in the cabin, the silence of sleeping passengers, charged the atmosphere with intimacy. "Will we be landing soon?"

"About a half hour. I hated to wake you, but I thought you'd want to get your bearings before we arrived."

She brushed her bangs from her eyes. As she settled in her seat, her elbow brushed his. Neither of them moved away. "Did you sleep?"

"No. I'm too wired. I can't believe I actually know where Karla and Stacey are. I'm afraid Arthur will wave a wand and they'll disappear again."

Now was the time to tell Adam what she knew. "There's a reason Mr. Carrero feels the way he does about you."

Adam sighed. "I know. I wanted to build a reputation on my own without him."

"That's not all of it." Her heart pounded. "Leona told him you were unfaithful. That you had an affair with your secretary."

Adam's brows drew together and his blue eyes shot silver sparks of anger. "I think your intuition is working overtime."

"This has nothing to do with my abilities, Adam. Mr. Carrero told me."

Adam's eyes narrowed and his arm went rigid on the armrest. "Why would he tell you that?"

"I was trying to convince him you had the girls' welfare at heart."

"And he was trying to prove to you what a jerk I am. Did he succeed?"

Her heart hurt, but she knew she had to ask the question for her own peace of mind. "Were you unfaithful when you were married to Leona?"

Adam's cheeks flushed and his hand balled into a fist. "Arthur has planted the doubt. I doubt if my denial will do any good since you had to ask the question."

She'd hurt him. She'd only met Adam two and a half weeks ago, yet in the time she'd known him, she'd come to trust him, to know he was an honorable man. So why had she needed to ask the question? Because Brian had been seeing his ex-wife behind her back? Probably. Obviously Adam wasn't the only one having a problem with trust.

When they arrived at Orly at seven-thirty in the morning French time, Adam rented a car to drive to Chinon. After studying a map, he calculated that they should get there around the lunch hour. There was a tension between him and Jana that had nothing to do with the long trip and everything to do with the question she had asked him.

As they drove through the French countryside, Jana lay her head against the back of the seat. Although she'd slept on the plane, she felt as if she hadn't slept for a week. But she couldn't nap now, not with the map on her lap. She did wish she and Adam could talk casually as they had so often before. But he wasn't in the mood for talking.

At one of the villages, Adam asked her if she'd like to stretch her legs. She knew he was anxious to get to their destination and appreciated his consideration. They stopped at a bakery, buying rolls and coffee.

Sitting in the car with the windows open, Jana finished a roll and decided to deal with the tension. "Adam, about Arthur's accusation. I..."

He'd tossed his suit coat in the back seat and rolled up his shirtsleeves. "Let's forget it. I only have one thing on my mind now. Nothing else matters." He pulled the map onto the armrest. "We'll be there in about two hours. Hopefully someone in Chinon will know where the estate is located."

But as soon as they drove into the town along the Vienne River with its cobbled streets and quaint houses, Jana didn't need directions. She guided Adam through town, past orchards, until they turned onto a lane leading to a gray stone house. It looked classic—more than large enough for a woman and two children. Poplars dotted the front lawn while willows swayed low along the side. A green-and-yellow sign hung to the right of the front door.

Adam spoke for the first time since she'd begun giving him directions. "How did you know?"

"I could hear Karla's and Stacey's voices. As if they were guiding me. I know it's crazy—"

He shook his head. "It doesn't seem crazy anymore."

They climbed the stone steps and Adam lifted the door knocker. A rotund woman with rosy cheeks and wearing a bright floral print dress answered the door. "*Monsieur? Mademoiselle?* May I help you?"

"I'm Adam Hobbs. Stacey and Karla's father. I'd like to see them."

"Oh, *mon dieu*. Ms. Carrero said if this ever happened—"

"Collette, who is it?"

"It's me, Leona," Adam called inside. "Let me in. Or so help me I'll get the French police involved in this."

Leona came to the door and put her hand on the older woman's arm. "It's all right, Collette."

Leona Carrero was more strikingly beautiful in person than she was in her photograph. Jana felt awkward and out of place.

Adam's ex-wife stepped back and said, "Come in, Adam. I knew it was only a matter of time." Her voice grew husky. "I made a mistake and—"

"You're damn right you did. Don't you even think about disappearing out the back door because this time I'll call the FBI and the state department."

Leona took a step away from him. "I'm just thankful you haven't called them in before now. Father gave me your message. Adam, I'm sorry. I was just so afraid if I came back, you'd take Karla and Stacey away from me."

He let Jana precede him into the foyer that was more the size of a living room. Then he turned to his ex-wife. "I'm taking them with me. Now."

Her gaze darted from him to Jana. "You can't just rip them away from me like this. That's not good for them."

"Being away from me for six months hasn't been good for them."

Jana knew she shouldn't interfere, but her concern for two little girls urged her to put her hand on his arm. "Adam, she's right. You don't want to scare them or—"

At that moment, Stacey and Karla ran into the foyer, saw Adam and stopped in their tracks.

He looked at them and smiled with such bittersweet joy that tears pricked Jana's eyes.

Holding out his arms to his daughters, he said, ''Hi. How about a hug?''

Stacey's eyes were as blue as Adam's, her wavy brown hair curled on her cheeks. She put one finger in her mouth, but came tentatively toward him. Adam enfolded her in his arms, then leaned away. ''I think you've grown two inches! And gotten a whole lot prettier.''

Stacey smiled.

He held his arms out to Karla. ''Come here and let me look at you.''

The four-year-old approached slowly but stood a good two feet from her father.

Jana felt for Adam. The look on his face was pained when he realized Karla didn't intend to come any closer. ''Karla, what's wrong?''

Sullenly she insisted, ''Nothin'.'' But she didn't come toward him.

Trying to ease the situation, Adam smiled. ''Your ponytail is longer. You've grown two inches, too.'' An awkward silence descended on the foyer until Karla pointed to Jana. ''Who's she?''

Jana stepped closer to both girls and crouched down to their level. ''I'm Jana Kellerhern. Your dad and I are friends.''

Stacey toddled right over to her and studied her face. ''Come plane?''

Karla translated. ''She wants to know if you came on an airplane.''

''Yes, we did.''

Keeping her eyes on Adam but speaking to Jana, Karla complained, ''It's a long ride. We colored and watched videos.''

''Did you come here in Arthur's plane?'' Adam asked Leona.

"Does that surprise you?" his ex-wife countered.

"No." Adam's mouth set in a tight line. Jana knew Adam's P.I. had checked airline manifests, unable to find Leona or the girls' names.

Leona looked at Jana, then Adam. "I'd expect you're both tired from traveling. Would you like to freshen up?" Her eyes were pleading as they begged Adam not to take the girls too quickly. "We've eaten lunch, but the cook can fix something for you."

Adam crouched down beside Jana and his daughters. Karla moved closer to her mother, away from him. "I'll bet you've gotten a whole batch of new toys since you've been here."

Stacey nodded.

"I'd like to see all of them, but I have to talk to your mom first. Could you keep Jana company for a little while?"

Karla reluctantly agreed. "I guess."

Jana said, "I particularly like dolls. Do you have any?"

Stacey nodded again and tugged Jana's hand. "C'mon. Show you."

Jana stood and as Stacey held her hand, Collette led her and the girls down a hall beyond the foyer. Jana felt an instant bond with these two little girls. If she could help them make the transition that was sure to come, she'd like to do it as their friend.

Stacey was an outgoing two-and-a-half-year-old who pointed and babbled to Jana the whole time she ran from toy to toy in the playroom, showing off first her dolls, then her stuffed toys. She pushed a white furry kitten into Jana's hands. "Muffin. Sleep wif her."

Jana smiled and held Muffin under her arm. "Karla, which toys are your favorites?"

The four-year-old went to a child-size table and chairs covered with blocks. "My goodest toys are at home. Grandfather sent these."

Jana sensed a melancholy in Karla. The little girl missed her home in L.A., her room at Adam's, as well as her friends and the people she was used to being with. "Do you like it here in France with your mom?"

"Everybody talks funny."

Jana didn't want to pump Karla for information. She just wanted the little girl to know if she wanted to talk, there was someone who would listen. "What do you build with your blocks?"

"Everything. Wanna build a zoo?"

"I'd like that. Tell me what you'd like to do and we can help you do it."

Stacey grinned at Jana, glad to be included.

At some point while they were building, Collette slipped out of the room. As Jana and Karla and Stacey were placing small plastic animals in their appropriate sections of the zoo, she returned.

"Do we have to take a nap today?" Karla asked. "Can't we play with Jana?"

Collette responded, "Mademoiselle Kellerhern has had a long journey. She would probably like some lunch and a rest herself. Remember, if you rest now, you can stay up later tonight."

"Where's Mommy?"

"She's still speaking with your father."

Karla frowned.

Collette turned to Jana. "I can show you to the kitchen. Jacqueline has prepared *salade* and sandwiches."

"Thank you. If you could show me where I can freshen up—"

"We'll show you the bathroom," Karla offered. "C'mon."

The girls went to their rooms while Jacqueline served Jana in the formal dining room. She felt silly sitting at the long table by herself. After a sorbet for dessert, she settled in a small sitting room off the foyer. Long casement windows flooded the room with afternoon sun on two sides. The yellow-white-and-green flowered sofa invited her to curl up and relax.

What were Leona and Adam talking about? What plans were they making? Were they simply talking? Jana shouldn't care, but she did. Too much. She yawned, feeling the fatigue of the time change. Laying her head against a pillow, she knew she was too tired to tell herself she shouldn't care.

"Jana?"

She awakened at the sound of Adam's voice close to her. When she opened her eyes, he towered over her. "What time is it?"

"Almost four."

So many questions flooded her mind, but she asked the most practical, the least risky. "Did you get lunch?"

"I just grabbed a sandwich. The girls will be down soon and I want to talk with them. I think Leona and I have everything straightened out."

Jana had a sudden vision of Adam and Leona embracing. Was that from the past? The present? The future? She swallowed hard. "What are you going to do?"

"If the girls agree, they're going to go home with me. I believe Leona was afraid, impulsively took the girls, but then was even more fearful of the consequences of coming back. I assured her that I have no intention of cutting her off from Karla and Stacey, that I only want joint custody and a say in their lives.''

"Adam, would you like a martini?" As Leona stood in the doorway, she saw Adam sitting beside Jana. "I'm sorry. I didn't mean to interrupt."

Jana was quick to assure her. "You're not."

Leona came forward and extended her hand. "We really haven't met. I know you helped find us for Adam."

Jana gave Leona's hand a brief shake, then started to rise from the sofa. Adam stilled her by placing his hand on her thigh. She might not have felt anything when she shook Leona's hand, but Adam's touch on her leg created a jumble of thoughts and sensations that were too difficult to sort through.

"Leona, your father gave Jana some information I'd like you to straighten out." Adam's voice was firm.

His ex-wife looked almost fearful for a moment. "What kind of information?"

"I think you know."

"Adam, I had to give him a good reason. Otherwise he would have blamed the failure of our marriage on me."

The lines along Adam's mouth creased deep with his frown. "Why? He's never liked me."

"Maybe not. But he respects you. He's never respected me. You know that. He doesn't listen to what I say. He tries to control my life."

"But it was your idea to run with the girls."

"Yes. He went along with it because of what I told him about you."

"Which was..."

Jana knew what Adam was doing. He wanted her to hear the truth and believe it. "Adam, you don't have to—"

"Yes, I do. Leona, what did you tell him?"

Leona squared her shoulders and met her ex-husband's hard stare. "I told him you were unfaithful. I was wrong to do that, too. Adam, I'm sorry. I know I have a lot to make up for."

Adam's voice held quiet certainty. "You have to stand up to your father sometime. You can't go through life trying to please him. I want you to set him straight. Understand?"

She sighed. "Yes. I know it's what I have to do. Soon." At the doorway, she turned back to them. "You will stay here, won't you? We have plenty of room. I know you want to spend the evening with the girls and tuck them in."

Adam squeezed Jana's knee with his fingers. "Is that all right with you?"

"I don't want to impose. I can stay in a hotel in Chinon."

Leona shook her head. "Nonsense. Collette has readied rooms for both you and Adam. Unless..." Her voice trailed off, suggesting they might want one room.

"That'll be fine," Adam responded.

Leona gave them a speculative look and left the room.

"You didn't have to do that," Jana murmured.

"I wanted the facts clear."

Jana tried to shrug off the feeling that he was still hurt she hadn't believed in him. "Leona seems very...nice." *Does she want you back?* a small voice cried.

But of course he didn't hear it. "Leona usually is nice. She's always tried to please everyone. And that's impossible. I think she's changed a lot in the past six months. Maybe it was being away from Arthur, or maybe it was having full responsibility for the girls.''

"They're wonderful children, Adam."

A grin eased the serious lines from his forehead. ''I think so.'' He took her chin in his hand, and his grin slipped away. "Thank you for finding them."

Adam's adrenaline was still pumping, chasing away the fatigue and tension of the past six months. Jana's doubt about his fidelity had niggled at him since she'd raised the question. He wasn't sure why it bothered him so. Showing her the truth had been all-important. But now, even that faded into the background as he gazed into her brown eyes.

Jana was such a giving woman, so confident in who she was. The softness of her lips, the tilt of her head, the expression in her eyes, pulled him toward her until his lips found hers. She warmed him. Each time he kissed her, the chill left his heart, and her giving response filled him with a pleasure that made him ache with wanting. As he deepened the kiss, all he wanted was to feel her surround him.

As before, she responded with a tentative innocence that made him wonder about her romantic past. She was a sensual, caring woman. Had her gift kept her isolated? More than once she'd hinted that had been the case. He wanted to erase that isolation as much as he wanted to appease his desire.

He stroked her mouth, nibbled on her lip, cradled her head in his hands, needing to bring her closer—

Jana tore away, putting a few inches between them on the sofa. "I can't do this." Her hand trembled as she lowered it to her lap. "Stacey, Karla, Leona..."

Something happened when he was around Jana— something unfamiliar, almost uncomfortable. Rational thought fled, and he got caught up in . . . her. "Maybe I should have told Leona we only need one room."

Looking astonished, Jana hopped up from the sofa. "I never gave you any indication that I was willing—"

"What was that kiss about, Jana, if not willingness?"

"It was...it was... I don't know. We've been thrown into this situation together. That doesn't mean I want to go to bed with you. And even if I did, it would be totally inappropriate . . . here. In fact, I wonder how you could even consider it. Do you have something to prove to Leona?"

As far as he was concerned, Leona didn't enter into this. "I don't have anything to prove. You and I both know there's an amazing chemistry between us."

"Chemistry soon fizzles out, Adam. Or do you and Leona still have chemistry working between you?"

"Leona and I have the girls between us. That's all."

"And a history," Jana reminded him with a frown.

"A history I'd rather forget." When his marriage broke up, he'd looked at his relationship with Leona. They really never had anything in common—not their goals, their vision of their future, or their dreams. He'd married her thinking she'd separate from her father. But she hadn't. And Adam's goal to succeed for them both had driven them apart. They'd made mistakes. Essentially they'd been wrong for each other from the beginning. Leona still believed material wealth was a sign of prestige. Adam had learned differently—integrity and a bond with his daughters was much more important than either wealth or prestige.

Jana brushed her bangs to the side, a gesture he'd noticed she used when she was nervous. "I'm going to find

Collette and see which room she'd like me to use. I'd like
to bathe or shower."

The idea of her doing either caused a tangible increase of his pulse. But she'd made herself clear. Kissing him was one thing. More than that was out of the
question. Here, anyway. What would happen when they
got back to L.A.? Would she go back to her life as a
manicurist? Or would she go back to Indiana?

Did it really matter? His focus had to be Karla and
Stacey. After all, he had his daughters back now. Why
should he be concerned about anything else?

Jana threw the catalogs she'd been studying onto the
table beside the sofa. Ordering craft supplies was the
farthest thing from her mind, though her mother had
reminded her for the past two weeks that Christmas
supplies were running low. Christmas supplies. She
didn't even know where she'd be at Christmas.

Right now, Adam, Leona, Karla and Stacey were dis-
cussing...something. And Jana felt shut out. Of course
she was shut out. She didn't belong in their plans.

Dinner had been strained, although they'd all tried to
carry the conversation. During a moment when Leona
had touched Adam's hand to make a point, Jana had
realized with startling clarity that she was jealous. Tum-
bling over that realization came the stunner—she was
falling in love with Adam Hobbs.

She'd denied it, analyzed it and told herself she had to
put distance between them. That would be easy once
they returned to L.A. Until then, she'd keep to herself
and stay away from him. How difficult could that be?

Hurried footsteps sounded on the floor in the hall.
Adam appeared in the doorway, a worried expression on
his face. "Have you seen Karla?"

Her heart hammered. "No. What's wrong?"

"Collette came down to tell us the girls were ready for bed. But when I went to Karla's room, she was gone."

Leona appeared next to him. "I can't find her anywhere. She knows she's not supposed to go outside by herself anytime, let alone at night. The river isn't that far away."

"Jana?" Adam was looking at her expectantly. "Can you help us?"

Leona broke the silence between them. "How can she help?"

Jana didn't think twice about picturing the dark-haired four-year-old. Karla had been quiet during dinner, watching Adam but not reaching out to him. Now as Jana thought about Adam's older daughter, she had the strong sensation that Karla *was* outside, but not in any danger.

"Ask Collette to check the house once more. You and Leona cover the front yard, I'll take the back."

Leona looked indignant. "Why should we do what you say?"

Adam kept silent. It was Jana's choice what she wanted to tell Leona.

Jana sighed. She was tired of keeping her gift under wraps. "I'm a psychic, Leona. That's why."

Chapter Seven

Jana brushed through the branches of an immense willow as she let her instinct guide her as well as the light of the flashlight. After her announcement, Leona had looked at Jana as if she were crazy. Not an unusual reaction.

But Adam had jumped in quickly, telling his ex-wife, "Jana led me here to the girls. I have no doubt she can find Karla now."

Leona had studied Jana closely, then said, "I'll talk to Collette."

Jana appreciated Adam's faith in her—it was satisfying. But it also frightened her. What if she couldn't find Karla?

For a moment all of her inner radar seemed to jam. Taking a few deep breaths of night air, she consciously relaxed and started walking again, stopping when she came to a border of trees along the river. They looked centuries old. She couldn't make out what kind they were in the dark.

An inner leading guided her to swing her flashlight in a huge arc. She saw Karla's profile as the child perched in the V of a tree about two feet off the ground. It reminded Jana of Karla's special place in Adam's backyard. She laid her flashlight at the base of the trunk so that Adam could see it, then following her instincts rather than the logic that told her she should call Adam and get the little girl inside out of the dark night, she leaned against the tree beside Karla.

Facing the same direction as the four-year-old, Jana silently studied the river illuminated only by a slip of a moon.

Karla shifted restlessly in her perch. "I don't wanna go in."

"Your mommy and daddy are worried about you." Jana let silence lay between them again.

"I *wanna* go home, but I'll miss Mommy."

Jana moved a little closer so her shoulder brushed Karla's, creating the physical contact Jana sensed the child needed. "Your mommy and daddy love you a lot."

"Why didn't Daddy come sooner?"

Jana understood the hurt in Karla's voice. "He couldn't find you."

The child's voice trembled. "He should have."

All the explanations in the world wouldn't help. Jana knew Karla had felt abandoned by Adam even though she was the one who'd gone away. Knowing the facts was one thing. Feeling the repercussions of them was another. Adam's daughter had missed him for six long months, and it would take time for that loss to heal.

She could only offer Karla reassurance. "Your daddy loves you very much. He missed you as much as you missed him. All he wants now is to play with you and talk with you and tuck you into bed at night.''

Karla laid her head against Jana's shoulder.

The gesture of trust tugged at Jana's heart, and she tilted her head against the child's. "He wants to make up for the time he's missed. Can you give him a chance to do that?''

She felt Karla's small I-don't-know shrug.

"Jana? Karla?" Adam's husky baritone floated to them from a few feet away. "We're fine," Jana assured him.

He called across the yard. "Leona. Over here.''

"He's gonna be mad," Karla murmured close to Jana's ear.

"Let me talk to him a minute." Jana turned toward Adam.

He said in a low voice, "You don't have to talk to me. I heard what she said. I just don't know what to do about it.''

His words near her ear were intimate and created more of a bond between them. But it was a bond that could hurt her. Although she wanted to keep her distance, she couldn't ignore his pain. "Give her time and love and she'll come around.''

Adam reached for his daughter. "Come here, honey. I'll lift you down.''

"I can do it myself.''

Jana heard Adam's sharp intake of breath and felt the rejection he experienced. She wished she could tell him that Karla would trust him again soon, that her anger would disappear. But she couldn't.

Karla climbed from the tree and touched her feet to the ground as Leona reached them. Bending, she hugged her daughter tightly. "Sweetheart, you could have gotten hurt out here alone at night. Promise me you'll never do that again."

Karla didn't answer.

Adam crouched down beside her, stroking her hair behind her ear. "Honey, what you did was dangerous. Running away never solves a problem. If something's wrong, I want you to tell me."

Karla averted her gaze from her father's.

He closed his eyes for a moment, and Jana hurt for him. Adam might want a reunion with his daughters, but Karla was going to fight him every step of the way.

"You want them to live with you for the summer?"

"It's only fair, Leona. You've had them exclusively for six months. I'm asking for half that time."

Leona walked to the edge of the patio and sat at a table under a blue-and-white striped umbrella. She wore a lime green sundress, her shoulders tan and bare in the heat of the afternoon. When Adam looked at her, he was still angry that she could have kept Karla and Stacey from him all those months. But that was all he felt. She was a beautiful woman, but no desire stirred. Not the way it did with Jana. There was still a bond with Leona because of the girls, but it wasn't the caring, intense bond that connected him to Jana. He couldn't explain the physical pull toward her or his acceptance of her gift. He simply knew Jana was honest, straightforward, and held no hidden agenda. She was so different from Leona. So much stronger.

"You hate me, don't you?" Leona asked in a faint voice.

"I hate what you did. I don't hate you."

"This wasn't Father's fault. I decided to take Karla and Stacey on my own. I was afraid if you sued for joint custody, eventually you'd want full custody. When you decided to be an involved father, Adam, you were good at it. They enjoyed their time with you so much, I thought they'd want to live with you."

Leona brushed her long hair away from her face, a gesture Adam had once found provocative. Now it didn't provoke anything but the knowledge that he had fallen for outside packaging, not the woman beneath the polished facade. Jana didn't have a facade. She was genuine, from the compassion glowing in her brown eyes to her honest responses to his questions and desires.

He dragged a chair from the table with his sneaker and sat across from his ex-wife. "Over the years I might have questioned your love for me, but I never questioned your love for the girls. They wouldn't want to live with me exclusively. They'd miss you too much."

Leona's eyes glistened with unshed tears. "I never should have married you. It wasn't fair to either of us. I cared about you, but I was rebelling against Father, too. And I never felt the grand passion that I know now—" She stopped abruptly as if she'd said too much.

Adam's first reaction was a sense of betrayal. But then he realized he hadn't felt "grand" passion, either. Maybe his ability to love had been too limited by his upbringing. Maybe he was never meant to love the way a man and woman should in a marriage. It sounded as if Leona had met someone who made the world tilt and bells ring. And he suspected who that someone was.

"I know about Jean Watteau."

Her mouth rounded and she snapped it shut. "Jana?"

He shook his head. "My private investigator. How serious is it?"

Leona hesitated and studied the tips of her pink nails. "I don't know. Yet. But I do know Jean makes me feel ... whole. You and I never did that for each other."

She was right. Emptiness had been with him ever since he was a small boy, as if something important had always been missing from his life. An unsettling thought hit him. "You're not going to move here, are you?"

"I'm taking one day at a time. Jean hasn't met Father yet..."

"Arthur would approve. From what I understand Watteau has the upbringing and the fortune your father would choose for you."

She raised her head. "I don't lov... like Jean for his upbringing or his money."

Adam leaned forward, knowing that the same way he had faced truths about his responsibility in the failure of their marriage, Leona needed to do the same. "Just as you have to stand up to Arthur someday, you have to be honest with yourself. Watteau's upbringing and fortune are as much a part of him as my background and work ethic are a part of me."

"You make me sound like a snob!"

Adam laughed, but without rancor or malice. "You are. You always have been."

She looked insulted for a moment, then smiled as the truth hit home. "I guess you're right."

He relaxed in his chair. "Think about letting me have the girls for the summer."

Leona searched his face, then nodded. "I will."

Jana heard the sound of Adam's laughter as she approached the double doors leading to the terrace, and her heart sank. Adam and Leona would always have a bond between them—their children. Were they realizing now that their divorce had been a mistake? That they belonged together?

The questions were too painful. Instead of interrupting the tête-à-tête on the terrace, she decided to go for a walk. Maybe even a jog. Yet she knew she couldn't run from the powerful feelings Adam evoked in her. Hurrying up to her bedroom, she changed into a tank top, running shorts and sneakers. She'd no sooner let herself out the front door when Karla called from the yard, "Jana? Come play with us."

Early this morning, she'd come downstairs to find Karla and Stacey in the playroom. Stacey, with her rosy cheeks and toddler grin, had plopped down next to Jana and asked her to read a story. Before Jana knew it, Karla had flipped off her baseball cap and was sitting on the other side of her. They'd read three books. Jana genuinely enjoyed spending time with the little girls.

Now Collette beckoned to her as well. When she came within speaking distance, Jana could see Collette's face was red from exertion. "I love taking care of children, but they need someone younger to run after the ball. Do you mind?"

Jana took the soccer-type ball from the older woman. "No. I can use the exercise." She dropped it to the ground and kicked it lightly toward Stacey.

Some time later, her own face hot from laughing, running and playing in the sun, she prepared to kick the ball, saw Adam standing behind Karla and missed.

Stacey jumped up and down. "Daddy, Daddy. Play?"

He smiled and looked at Karla. "Is that all right with you?"

"I guess," his older daughter mumbled as she repositioned the bill of her cap.

The sun shone on Adam's brown hair, picking up reddish strands. His navy polo shirt and shorts showed his athletic physique to perfection. At Karla's less-than-enthusiastic response, his smile flagged, and Jana wanted to brush the worry from his brow. Keeping her distance was more difficult than she ever imagined it would be.

With Adam involved in the game, it got faster. He was gentle with Karla and ran after Stacey when she scooted after the ball, picking it up and squealing with delight. As she tried to run away with it, he caught her, tickled her and tossed the ball back into play. When he shot it to Jana, his sly smile and quick reflexes forced her to keep her mind on the game. Karla kicked the ball to Jana. Jana ignored Adam and kicked it back to Karla. Not quite ready, Karla propelled it with the side of her foot. Jana went for it and collided into Adam as his foot made contact with the ball.

Her breath whooshed out of her as his shoulder connected with hers, and his arm went around her to steady her. She looked up into his eyes and started shaking. He was holding her protectively, but there was nothing protective in the blue of his gaze. It was as steamy as the two of them emanating heat and desire the longer they held on to each other.

Collette's voice penetrated the haze surrounding them. "Karla. Stacey. It's time to go in for a snack and a rest. Come. Come."

As Karla grumbled, Adam dropped his arm from around Jana and suggested, "Maybe we can play again later this evening. Your mom might want to join us."

"She won't play. She doesn't like to get her hair messed up," Karla said as she approached her father with the ball.

"We can play again even if she doesn't want to."

Karla's enthusiasm for the game seemed to wane and she shrugged.

As the girls went inside with Collette, he watched them and rubbed the back of his neck. Jana knew he did that when he was worried or frustrated. Finally he turned to her and asked, "Would you like to go for a walk?"

Being close to him now would be a mistake. "I'd better not. I could use a rest, too."

With the determination she'd learned was part of his nature, he took her by the elbow and guided her to the side of the house under the shade of the trees. "I can understand Karla's withdrawal. But I don't understand yours. What's wrong, Jana? Something has changed between us."

She made herself meet his eyes and steeled herself against their power. "Nothing has changed, Adam. We haven't known each other very long. In a different place, with different people, we're different."

"I don't buy it."

His lawyer's stare was probing and unsettling, so much so she blurted out, "I feel like an intruder. You and Leona have a history."

He took Jana by the shoulders. "So we have a history. What of it?"

"Karla and Stacey probably want you to get back together again. Kids always do."

The pressure on her shoulders increased slightly, though he kept his hold gentle. "Leona and I have talked to them about the divorce and told them it's not their fault. They know we're not going to live together anymore."

But what about the love? Jana's heart shouted. She couldn't ask.

He must have seen the questions in her eyes. "Leona and I are divorced, Jana. That's that."

Brian had been divorced, too.

Adam cupped her cheek in his hand. "Finding the girls doesn't mean you and I have to go our separate ways when we get back."

She wanted to sway toward him, wind her arms around his neck. But her cautious self, the part of her betrayed by Brian told her if they didn't go their separate ways, she'd get hurt. "I might be going home to Indiana soon."

His lips came closer to hers, and he murmured, "Then we should take advantage of the time we have."

Was it that simple? Why did she need to look into the future? Why did she want forever?

The questions stopped when he claimed her mouth. His lips moved hungrily over hers, as if they knew hers, as if they needed hers, as if they understood she wanted him as much as he wanted her. But wanting could never be enough, could it?

That question was silenced, too, by Adam's arms enfolding her until she was tight against him. He was so strong and...lovable. She didn't think he knew that. He was so hard on himself. He didn't know how good a father he was, or how good a husband he could be. Whether he knew it or not, he'd changed as he'd developed a relationship with his daughters. This man could never ignore his children, even in the drive to give them the best of everything. Because now he knew the best he could give them couldn't be bought, or earned, or judged by the income he made. He could only give them his best by giving them time and love.

His hand slipped under Jana's tank top, and she couldn't suppress a moan or the need she'd tried to ignore. She felt his shudder as his fingers met her bare skin, and for the first time in her life she felt as if she had power over a man. Adam wanted her—Jana Kellerhern. He knew about her "gift" and seemed to accept it as no one else in her life had.

But if she had power over him, he had just as much power over her. He scrambled her thoughts and emotions, renewed childlike dreams, awakened desires she'd never known were a part of her. His lips and tongue and hands aroused an unknown hunger that frightened her because it was strange and new, deep and primal. She strained against him, eager to discover why.

His hand left her back and passed over her midriff. When he backed away slightly, she wanted to protest until his fingers traced the cup of her bra and she trembled from the intensity of the sensations surging through her. Her heart raced, her body ached, her nipple hardened in expectation of more. His long fingers passed over her breast and...

"Adam! Adam. Father's on the phone. He wants to talk to you." Leona's voice was strong and clear as it soared to the side of the house from the front porch.

Adam stepped back and swore. Jana couldn't bear to look at him as she turned away and straightened her top, her heart still pounding, her body still trembling.

He clasped her shoulder. "Jana..."

"Go," she whispered. "It's important." She felt rather than saw his hesitation.

As Leona called for him again, he left Jana by the side of the house and headed for the porch.

For a moment, Jana had let herself believe this time could be different. For a moment, she'd let herself dream again. How foolish. And how painful.

* * *

Keeping to herself, Jana went for a walk, showered, then sat in her room reading a magazine she'd bought at the airport. Paging through was probably a better definition. Reading seemed beyond her level of concentration. When a heavy rap sounded on the door, butterflies danced in her stomach. She threw the magazine on the table beside the chair and opened her bedroom door.

Adam had changed, too. He'd rolled the sleeves of the soft chambray shirt to his elbows. His jeans pulled tight across his thighs, and she had to bring her gaze to his with an effort. Thinking about his body pressed against hers, his lips on hers, his hand on her breast... She swallowed hard.

"Can I come in?"

She could see the bed out of the corner of her eye. "That's not a good idea."

"Jana, I need to talk to you. About leaving. I'd like to fly out tomorrow."

She took a few steps back into the room and clasped her hands in front of her. "You've talked to Leona about it?"

He came into the room and closed the door. "And the girls. Leona's going to stay here for another week or so. She wants to pack up and get her affairs in order."

Jana glanced at the closed door, then at Adam who seemed to take up most of the space let alone the oxygen. "How do the girls feel about it?"

Digging his hands into his pockets, he sighed. "They seem okay. Karla's still not saying much, at least not to me. I'm hoping that will change once we're back in L.A. I'll take off the next two weeks to spend with them." He paused. "They were asking for you a little while ago."

Adam's jeans were worn white at provocative places.
She felt her cheeks growing hot as she pictured him in a
bathing suit, as she pictured him... "I needed time to
myself."

Not letting her off the hook, he persisted, "Because
of what happened earlier?"

She blew out a breath and went over to the window,
opening it wider. "Because of lots of things. How did
your call go with Mr. Carrero?"

"You're changing the subject," he said to her back.

Straightening the folds of the curtain, she responded,
"To an important one considering your history with
him. Unless you don't want to discuss it."

"Leona told him the truth about our divorce. He
wanted me to know he wouldn't interfere in my work
again."

Jana faced him. "The Sheffield-Babbock merger?"

"Yes. He didn't apologize. That's not Arthur's style.
But he did say he'd right the matter." Adam took a step
closer to her. "Jana..."

Panicking, she went to the closet and pulled out her
suitcase. "I'd better start packing."

His voice was husky. "You didn't bring that much."

"I don't like to wait until the last minute."

"It will soon be time for dinner."

"Have the girls call me." Lifting her suitcase onto the
bed, she unzipped it and avoided Adam's gaze. She
heard him open and close the door, then she sat down on
the bed, wishing she could see her own future, trying to
convince herself she hadn't fallen in love.

On the plane the next day, Adam helped Stacey get
settled in the seat by the window, fitting a Walkman on
her head so she could listen to a favorite tape. He turned

to help Jana, but found she and Karla had already settled in the two seats in the middle aisle.

He was grateful the girls had taken to Jana so easily. He was grateful to her for a lot of things. Maybe that's what the passion was all about—a good dose of chemistry mixed with gratitude. Potent stuff. Maybe she was right to back off. But her remoteness didn't feel right. For a man who'd never known how to be close to a woman, he wanted the closeness back that they'd experienced while they were putting together clues, facing Arthur, searching.

"That man's not at his window. Can I sit there?" Karla asked in a voice that carried through the business class cabin.

Adam was about to release his seat belt when the gentleman in question, dressed in a Western snap-button shirt, jeans and tooled boots, looked over at Jana and Karla and smiled. Adam recognized the look as the man's gaze passed over Jana. He was interested.

The man stood and invited Karla and Jana to move to the window seat. "I do this often. You'll get a lot more pleasure watching the clouds than I will."

Jana released her seat belt. "You're sure you don't mind?"

"Not at all," he drawled in a Texas accent thick enough for a Frenchman to recognize it.

Adam openly eavesdropped as the seat exchange took place and the man placed his Stetson on the empty cushion beside him. After Jana had buckled herself in, the man offered her his hand and introduced himself. Jana reciprocated. The man held Jana's hand much too long, in Adam's estimation. He was also much too friendly as he made conversation with her until they took off. She didn't seem remote or flustered with him. In fact, she looked enamored as the Texan described some of the sights he'd visited in Paris.

Adam couldn't hear Jana's responses, but he could see the animation on her face as she spoke. His gut twisted. How could she be so friendly to someone she'd just met? Didn't she know better? The guy looked all right. About his own age. About as tall. Of course, add the damn hat—

Jana laughed at something the man said. Adam would know that lilting sound anywhere. She hadn't laughed much around him. But then they hadn't had much to laugh about. Now...

Now what? She'd backed off. The girls were staying with him. Time alone with Jana would be practically impossible. And if they had time alone, then what? Jana had made it clear she wasn't interested in sex. He didn't have more to offer than a physical relationship. Trust was too much of an issue. Look at what he was feeling now. Jealousy. Pure and simple. If that guy patted Jana's arm one more time...

By the time they reached New York, Karla and Stacey had napped but were restless, bored and cranky. Adam felt unsettled and downright cranky, too, but told himself the car and plane ride wore on adults as well as children. After they went through customs, he picked up Stacey and carried her. She laid her head on his shoulder. Her arms around his neck took away his fatigue from the trip. He had his daughters with him again. Karla held Jana's hand, and he wished he could carry her as well, but he knew she wouldn't let him even though her eyelids were as droopy as her sister's.

Adam waited for Jana to come up beside him. "The girls did better than I expected. I thought about staying in New York overnight, but they'll probably sleep on the flight to L.A. I think they'd rather wake up tomorrow at home."

Before Jana could answer, the Texan came up to her, tipping his hat and giving Adam a short but acknowledging nod. "I don't want to keep you. I just want to tell you what a pleasure it was passing the time with you." He handed her a business card. "You ever decide you want to bring your craft shop down to Austin or even sell a franchise, you just let me know. I'd be honored to be an investor."

Jana took the card and tucked it into her purse. "Thank you, Charlie. I'll remember that. You have a good trip home."

His smile was pure Texas charm, his drawl dripped with the interest evident in his eyes. "And if you ever need anything else or just want to chat, you give me a call then, too. You hear?"

Adam couldn't listen to any more. He took Karla's hand and hitched Stacey higher in his right arm. To Jana, he said, "We'll be over at the hot dog stand when you're through."

Jana's expression was perplexed, but she nodded.

As Adam bought sodas for the girls, turmoil bubbled inside him, and he wished he hadn't declined the Scotch on the flight to New York.

Jana caught up with them a few minutes later. She attempted to make conversation, but he simply didn't feel like talking. When they boarded the plane, the girls wanted to sit together. Adam and Jana settled them with pillows and blankets and as soon as they could recline their seats, Karla and Stacey were asleep.

Next to Jana, Adam lay his head against the headrest and stared straight ahead. "Maybe you shouldn't be so friendly."

"Pardon me?" Jana's voice was tired. He felt her elbow nudge his arm as she turned toward him.

He straightened as he remembered her smiles, the Texan's. "Don't play innocent. You and Charlie. What do you know about him? I hope you didn't give him *your* business card."

"I don't *have* business cards."

"Did you give him your number?" Adam pressed.

"Is it any of your business?" she snapped with uncharacteristic sharpness.

"I'm concerned, that's all. You can't flirt with a stranger—"

"I *wasn't* flirting!" Her brown eyes were wide with astonishment, and she sounded hurt.

He tried to make his voice even and tempered. "It sure looked like it to me."

"Well, maybe you're not seeing clearly."

The hurt was gone and angry gold sparks had taken its place. What did she have to be angry about? "He was handsome, smooth and probably rich. Why wouldn't you flirt with him?"

She gripped the armrest tightly and lowered her voice. "Adam, I don't know what your problem is. I passed time with a fellow traveler on a long trip. If you had been sitting next to me and started a conversation, I would have talked to you."

Her explanation didn't erase the evidence of interest in the Texan's eyes. "Are you going to call him?"

"Maybe. If I'm ever in Texas," she added in a dry tone.

"Did you tell him?"

"What?"

"That you're a psychic."

"No!"

For some reason that one emphatic denial calmed Adam. "At least you don't confide in strangers."

"You were a stranger, but I confided in you," she murmured.

"I needed your help."

"I told you more than I tell most people."

Suddenly a question burned hotter than any question he'd ever asked. "Why?"

Her answer was slow in coming. "I don't know."

It wasn't the answer he wanted, though he didn't know what that was. Any more than he knew why jealousy had taken hold of him while Jana spent the trip talking to the Texan. If he could understand the jealousy, then maybe he could understand why his daughters going home with him wasn't enough to ease the restlessness and frustration of the past six months. Maybe he was having a delayed reaction to finding them.

Or maybe he was concerned that Jana would disappear from his life as quickly as she'd entered it.

Chapter Eight

Adam opened the door to his house and deactivated the alarm. Karla ran in front of him and up the stairs. He chuckled as he lowered Stacey to the floor and she toddled up the stairs after her sister. He watched to make sure she made it to the top. "It's hard to believe they were asleep a few minutes ago."

"It'll take a day or so until they adjust to the time change."

"You could stay tonight and help them settle in." He told himself he only had his daughters' welfare at heart, that he didn't care one way or the other if Jana stayed.

"I don't think that's a good idea. I'll just be an interference. They need time alone with you, especially Karla."

He could see the wisdom in Jana's refusal, but he also sensed she was still retreating from him. He didn't want that. "Maybe you're right. But I do think they'd like to see you again. Will you come on a picnic with us tomorrow evening?"

She hesitated.

He didn't want to chase her off, and he wasn't sure what would make her stay. Yet he couldn't keep from touching her cheek, from feeling satisfaction at the way desire sparkled in her eyes. "Jana, I want to see you, too."

She let out a soft sigh. "All right."

"We'll pick you up and drive up the coast. The girls have a favorite picnic area. The view is terrific."

Backing away from his hand, she said, "I might go into the salon for a while tomorrow if they need me. I'll call you and let you know what time I'll be finished."

He wanted to pull her into his arms and kiss her, he wanted to carry her upstairs to his bedroom. But he knew neither, right now, would be a good idea. He had daughters to care for, and Jana needed some time to decide to let him into her life. He was hoping he could hurry that decision.

Adam pushed Karla's stroller down the street at Disneyland, glancing at Jana as she pushed Stacey's, all the while thinking about last night's picnic. It had been . . . fun. Jana was fun—and warmth and smiles and sunshine. With the girls ever present, she seemed to be able to relax with him. When they touched inadvertently, she seemed comfortable, maybe because she knew nothing else could happen with the girls nearby. Being close to her, yet not so close was driving him crazy.

Even here.

This was Jana's first visit to Disneyland. She was as wonderful to watch as his daughters as her eyes widened, her smile broadened and she pointed out attractions she'd like to see.

Stacey turned around in her stroller. "Go potty."

"Me, too," Karla added from hers.

Adam pushed Karla's stroller toward the bathrooms as Jana guided Stacey's. "I'll get us something to drink and meet you back here in a few minutes. Think you can handle both of them?" Adam asked Jana, not knowing how she'd feel about caring for his daughters.

She simply smiled and helped Stacey from her stroller. "No problem."

One of the things he liked about Jana the most was her ability to take life in stride. She didn't get ruffled easily and her calmness calmed him, too. The line at the drink stand was long, but Adam decided to wait. Finally the vendor put the drinks in a cardboard carrier, and Adam headed back to meet Jana and the girls. He was striding toward the rest rooms when he saw Karla standing alone a few yards in front of them in the midst of the milling crowd. She looked upset and tears trickled down her cheeks.

When she saw him, she cried, "You weren't here!"

Jana came running with Stacey on her hip. "Karla, you should have stayed with us." To Adam, she said, "I was washing Stacey's hands and all of a sudden Karla was gone."

His four-year-old looked up at him accusingly. "You said you'd be here."

Adam set the box of drinks on the ground and crouched down beside his older daughter. "I *am* here. The line was longer than I expected."

She stared at the toes of her sneakers.

"Karla, you're going to have to trust me." He gently lifted her chin and vowed, "I promise if you get lost or you need me, I will find you. It might take some time. But I *will* find you."

His daughter stared into his eyes, searching for the proof that he'd keep his vow. Finally she murmured, "It took you a long time."

He knew she was referring to their trip to France. "I know. And I'm sorry."

She hesitated a moment, then said, "Mommy told Collette Jana helped you."

He didn't want to get into this here, but with Karla finally talking to him, he didn't want to stop her now. "Jana has a special gift. She can help find lost people."

Karla asked Jana, "You helped Daddy find us?"

"Yes, I did."

"How?"

"When I sat in your room among your things, when I talked to your grandfather, I felt and saw pictures that helped us find you."

Adam brushed the streak of a tear from his daughter's cheek. "It's an unusual talent. Not something Jana tells everyone about."

"Like a secret?"

Jana smiled. "Sort of like a secret. I only tell people who really need my help."

"Daddy needed your help." Karla threw her arms around Adam's neck and held him tight. "I'm glad you found us."

Emotion tightened Adam's chest. When Karla let go, he gave her another hug, then picked up the drinks.

Jana's eyes glistened, and his felt suspiciously moist. As they fetched the strollers and walked toward the shade of a palm, Jana said, "I wish I'd had a father like you."

"I messed up big at first. Don't make me into something I'm not."

They settled the girls in the shade with their drinks. Karla and Stacey were entranced watching Mickey Mouse amble down the street like a pied piper.

Jana was standing close enough to Adam for him to smell her shampoo mixed with sunshine. "Adam, for what it's worth, I think you've changed from the man you were. Agreed, I didn't know you then. But I know what I see now. You're a loving father and a good one. Don't doubt that for a minute. You put Karla's and Stacey's needs before yours. That's what parenting is all about."

Jana gazed at him with respect and admiration and maybe more. She made him feel as if he could climb the highest mountain or swim the deepest sea. He was attracted to her on such an elemental level, he ached. "Do you know what I want to do right now?"

"What?"

He lowered his voice and bent close so that only she could hear. "Kiss you and touch you until satisfying my needs and yours are the only thoughts we have."

She looked astonished for a moment; then he saw the flames of passion that licked inside of him dancing in her eyes. "Adam . . ."

He curled his arm around her, resting his hand on her waist. "You can't deny your feelings any more than I can."

The flames died down and she retreated again. "I can't deny them, but I have to be sure if I act on them."

He squeezed her waist, his hand temptingly close to her breast, his lips almost caressing her ear. "Sure of what? Why can't we simply enjoy each other?"

She leaned away. "Because I don't need a fling, Adam."

His heart beat at least three times before he asked, "What do you need?"

"I need a man who can give me his love for a lifetime."

Love. Such a small word. It hurt Adam. It brought up feelings of betrayal and abandonment. He took his arm from around her. Suddenly he knew Jana was right to keep her distance because he couldn't provide forever; he wasn't sure anybody could.

Adam tried not to call Jana. And he managed it for five whole days. But then Jon asked him and the girls to spend an afternoon at the beach. Adam picked up the phone and called Jana because he couldn't imagine *not* asking her along.

The sky was summer blue and cloudless, the ocean tumultuously gentle, the waves lapping at the shore with wide brushes of foam. Jana sat on the beach with Karla and Stacey, shoveling sand into a bucket to mold a tower for their castle. Her hair glowed blond in the bright sun. She was unmindful of the breeze and the smudge of sand on her cheek as she laughed with the girls and added water to her sand mixture from a bucket beside Stacey. Her bare shoulders and bare legs distracted Adam enough that he'd stopped helping for the time being so he could cool off with a soda.

Jon handed him one from the cooler on the beach towel. "She seems so ordinary," Jon commented. "When you told me she was a psychic—"

"She's not ordinary by a long shot. Jana's the most intuitive person I've ever met. Or maybe I just never met anyone like her before. She has this way of zeroing in on problems, or feelings. I don't know if Karla would have come around without her."

"She's good with the girls," Jon said blandly.

"They like her a lot."

"So do you."

Adam shot a warning look at his friend.

But Jon didn't take heed. He lowered his voice so it didn't carry on the breeze. "What's wrong with admitting you like a woman?"

"Don't read more into this than there is."

"Exactly what is there? She helped find the girls. Why are you still seeing her?"

"There's chemistry between us."

"Women have attracted you before and you haven't brought them along to build sand castles with your daughters."

"I told you I'm grateful to her for—"

Jon grunted. "Don't lie to yourself, Adam. You might want to take her to bed, but I think there's more going on than chemistry and gratitude."

"A bachelor is advising me on relationships?" Adam took a few long swigs of soda.

"Look. I got burned last time around, but that doesn't mean I didn't learn something from it."

Adam's silence told Jon he wanted him to back off. But they'd been friends for too many years. "I know you, Adam. I know what you've gone through with Leona and her father and the girls. Just because you made a mistake once, doesn't mean you'll make it again. You've changed over the past two years."

Jana had told him the same thing. Maybe he had changed. But what had he changed into? A man who cared about his daughters, certainly, but what else? He'd focused on his girls and his work. He'd closed out everyone except Jon. He'd lost his belief in marriage because obviously he hadn't known how to *be* married. He'd lost trust in the power of love because he'd never felt its power, and now he wondered if it had any.

He believed in what he could touch and feel and see, not in some dream. He'd changed, all right. He'd become realistic. Yet when he looked at Jana, held her, kissed her... Hell! Gratitude and hormones didn't add up to anything more than sentimentality. He'd better separate them, and he'd better do it fast.

Finishing the soda, he crunched the can in his palm and tossed it into the trash bag on the towel. He heard Karla ask Jana, "Can we stay up till you leave tonight?"

Jana responded with a smile. "If you can keep your eyes open."

Adam straightened. "Jana, I'd appreciate it if the girls need permission for something they ask me. You're not their mother."

Jon muttered something under his breath. A wave broke on the shore, then another. Gulls screeched. And everyone stayed perfectly still, except Stacey, who shoveled sand into her bucket.

Then Jana spoke. "I'm well aware of that, Adam. I'm sorry if I overstepped my bounds." Her voice was soft but carried like a sonic boom. For a moment, her eyes grew shiny. She ducked her head and went to her beach towel, rummaging in her bag for something.

As soon as the words were out of his mouth, Adam had known he'd made a mistake. The hurt in Jana's eyes proved it.

Jon boldly stepped into the awkwardness. "Adam, why don't you finish the sand castle with the girls. Jana and I will go to the house and get supper started."

Stacey piped up, "Windows, Daddy. Do windows."

His daughter's speech had improved vastly in six months. He couldn't believe she was directing him in how to build the sand castle. But right now he felt as if he were standing on ground even less stable than sand. Adam glanced at Jana, but she was still rummaging in her bag. He sat down next to Stacey and poked a window into one of the sand mounds.

Jon patted Jana's shoulder. "C'mon. Let's go up to the house."

Jana slowly came to her feet. If she concentrated on putting one foot in front of the other, her tears wouldn't blind her. Adam couldn't have hurt her more if he'd slapped her.

Jon seemed to understand that Jana needed time to compose herself as they climbed the steps, walked through the yard and went into the kitchen. Jana stood inside the door, not sure what to do next.

Jon poured two glasses of lemonade and took them to the table. "Adam didn't mean what he said."

Jana felt her skin cooling in the air-conditioned house and shivered. "He sounded as if he did."

Jon shook his head and sat down. "He's fighting having feelings again."

Jana sank into a chair across the table. "He loves his daughters."

"There's no doubt about that. But I'm talking about feelings for you. Can I ask you something?"

She nodded.

"How do you feel about Adam?"

"I feel too much, and I wish I didn't," she said in a low voice.

"Why?"

"Because once before I fell in love with a man who had an ex-wife in the wings. They reconciled. I had become close to his son..." Jana shook her head.

"You think Adam and Leona will get back together?"

"It's possible."

Jon took a few swallows of lemonade. "From what I know of Adam and Leona, I can't see it. Maybe you're telling yourself they might get back together because you're afraid of taking a risk as much as Adam is."

Jana thought about it. Yes, she was afraid to commit to a man again, especially a man who couldn't make a commitment to her. "I don't even know if I'm going to stay in L.A."

"What if Adam asks you to stay?"

If Adam asked her to stay, it would be a sign that he did care about her. The problem was she wanted more than caring. She wanted love and commitment and forever. If he asked her to stay? "I'd stay." She pushed her glass back and forth on the table. "Have I overstepped my bounds with the girls?"

"No! It's obvious they like you. They turned to you so naturally. You're not doing anything wrong, Jana. Both you and Adam simply have to come to terms with what's happening between you and decide whether or not you're willing to take some risks."

"You've given me a lot to think about." She pushed her chair back. "Maybe I should talk to Adam about the girls."

Jon motioned to their glasses. "Finish your lemonade. It won't hurt Adam to stew awhile."

"Jon!"

"Well, it won't." He gave Jana a sly smile. "He put himself in the doghouse, let him sit there until after supper."

"But..."

Jon's smile vanished. "Jana, he needs some time. Trust me."

What did she have to lose? This was where the risk-taking started. If she loved Adam, she'd better get used to it.

Jana hated the awkwardness between her and Adam as well as the tension. Throughout supper they'd avoided each other's eyes. As he'd flown a kite with Karla, she'd entertained Stacey and stayed out of his way. But now with the sun setting, and Karla and Stacey ensconced in front of the television with a Disney video, the silence between them was obvious.

Jon asked, "How about a game of cards?"

Adam stood. "Actually I'd like to stretch my legs before we leave. Jana, would you like to go for a walk on the beach?"

The question came as a surprise. All evening, Jana had thought Adam wanted to get away from her, not spend time with her. "But the girls..."

"Will be fine where they are," Jon reassured her. "I'll bet in five minutes they'll be curled up on the floor asleep. I'll be here with them. You two go."

Adam went to his daughters and told them he and Jana were going for a short walk.

Karla asked, "And Uncle Jon is staying here?"

"Yes. We'll be back before the video is over."

"Promise?"

He gave his daughter a tight hug. "I promise."

Stacey wanted a hug, too, although her eyes were droopy. Adam kissed both his daughters, then waited until they were settled on the rug.

As he crossed to Jana, he checked his watch. "I want to make sure we're back."

Jana said softly, "We will be."

As they walked down the stone steps, Adam took her arm. She remembered the last time they'd been here. He had been preoccupied with finding his daughters, and she'd realized how attracted she was to him. The breeze blew her tiered peasant skirt around her legs. The full short sleeves of her blouse wafted around her arms.

Adam guided her to the edge of the shore where they could walk more easily. They strolled in silence, the night sounds of the ocean emphasizing the gulf between them. Abruptly Adam stopped. "I'm sorry."

Tears pricked Jana's eyes, and she tried to blink them away. The emotion they brought with them stuck in her throat, making her voice husky. "I don't know what you want from me, Adam."

With a groan of frustration, he roughly pulled her into his arms and crushed her mouth with his. He was hungry and demanding. The gentleness he usually exhibited had no part in his kiss. But the wildness of it ignited the primitive yearning in Jana. She accepted his tongue as it darted against hers, swept her mouth, then retreated only to invade again. Her breath caught as he cupped her bottom and thrust provocatively against her. It happened so fast she had no time to erect defenses or guard her heart.

As suddenly as he'd pulled her into his arms, he released her. Though he'd dropped his hands, he stood close enough that she could feel his breath on her mouth still wet from his kiss. It was an exciting sensation, al-

most as exciting as the passion in his eyes catching the
light of the moon and stars.

"I suppose I should apologize for that, too."

Her hands trembled, but she reached out and took
another risk by stroking his jaw. "Not if it was as honest as it felt."

He took her hand and held it to his cheek, his expression pained. "Honest. What an unusual word for a kiss.
Maybe it's the first honest kiss I've ever given. I don't
know what I want from you, Jana. You're like one of
those stars up there, burning with life and compassion
and gifts I can't begin to understand. I'm almost afraid
to touch you, but I can't seem to stay away."

The turmoil in his voice told her he *was* feeling again.
But she didn't know if one of those feelings was love.
"Do you want me to back off from the girls?"

"No!" He kissed her palm, and shivers skipped up
her arm. "This afternoon I was taking my confusion out
on you. You've been so good to them and for them.
They need someone besides me and Leona. They need
you as a friend. So do I."

"A friend, Adam?"

He ran his thumb sensuously along her lower lip. "A
very good friend."

Adam wanted more than friendship and they both
knew it. But how much more?

Sunday evening, water splashed Jana in the face. She
raised her head and saw Stacey grinning at her as the little girl played in the shallow end of the pool with inflat-
able floats on her arms. "Hey, you. Maybe I don't want
to be a fish like you."

Stacey giggled and splashed Jana again. In the deep
end, Adam tossed a sponge ball to Karla. She captured

it and threw it to Jana. Jana caught it above her head just as the phone rang.

"I'll get it. Karla, go over to the shallow end with Jana." As Adam vaulted onto the patio with the ease and strength of an athlete, Karla swam toward Stacey.

After their walk on the beach last night, Adam had invited Jana to come today for supper and a swim. She knew she was tempting heartache, but she loved being with him and his daughters.

Jana looked up at him as he picked up the wireless phone. His gaze held hers and he gave her a smile that weakened her knees. The smile disappeared as he listened to the person on the other end of the line.

Adam motioned Jana to the phone. She couldn't imagine who could want to talk to her.

When she reached Adam, he handed her the wireless. "Shane Walker."

Her heart beat faster as she said, "Hello?"

"Jana, I need your help."

"My help?"

"I just got a call from a friend. His daughter disappeared this afternoon. They live in the canyons. She's four. Apparently her mother was taking a nap and she managed to unlock the door and go outside. Her parents are frantic. A search party has been combing the area for the last few hours but with darkness falling, her father is desperate. Can you drive up here and see what you can do?"

"Mr. Walker..."

"I know how you helped Adam. I know how you've helped others. It's a little girl. She's probably hungry and getting cold."

Compassion, guilt, the need to use her gift to help someone filled her as they always did. She remembered

the night when Karla had gone outside on her own. And
as usual, she couldn't say no. "Give me directions."

Although he'd been keeping his eyes on his daughters, Adam heard her and reached for the legal pad and
pen on the table next to him. Jana took them and scrib-
bled down the location. "Who should I look for once I
get there?"

Adam listened as Jana asked appropriate questions
getting the information she needed. She was methodical
and matter-of-fact, and he realized she'd done this many
times before.

When she switched off the phone, she said, "I have to
get changed and go."

"I want to go with you."

"No, you don't. You'd have to sit somewhere, waiting, for who knows how long. It's almost the girls' bed-
time."

He scowled. "I could call Jon."

Her gaze drifted from his lips to his bare chest, and
she knew she had to tell him the truth. "Adam, you
won't be any help and you might even hinder what I have
to do. I have to stay focused on this little girl and if
you're there, that might be harder to do."

He stroked her cheek. "I'm glad I distract you. But I
don't like letting you go alone. You're sure you'll be all
right?"

"Mr. Walker will be there. I'll be fine."

"Come back here when it's over."

"Adam, I'll probably be tired . . ."

"Come back here." His blue eyes searched her face,
and he stood very still as he waited for her answer.

Softly she said, "I'll come here. But don't wait up. I
don't know when I'll be back."

* * *

As Jana followed the directions Shane Walker had given her, she thought about Adam's request and smiled. Maybe this time she could follow her heart without getting hurt. Maybe this time... But she remembered Adam's question at Disneyland. *Why can't we simply enjoy each other?* And he hadn't responded when she answered that she wanted a man who could love her for a lifetime. Did his nonresponse mean he couldn't do it?

She knew Adam was capable of that kind of love. But did he know he was?

Jana reached the address on the slip of paper beside her and stepped into chaos. It was always like this—cars parked every which way, people milling around, reporters with cameras held at bay on the front lawn. Jana stood on the edge of a group of technicians setting up by a mobile van and listened.

"Damn shame they didn't find her before dark."

"Yeah. It might be too late. You know how these things go. What if she's not lost? What if someone took her?"

As unobtrusively as possible, Jana slipped in and out among the bystanders and went around to the back of the house. She knocked and immediately someone answered. The man was tall, about thirty, good-looking with a well-defined jaw, long tawny hair and piercing brown eyes.

He gave her a swift appraisal. "Jana?"

"Yes. Mr. Walker?"

He opened the screen door for her. "Shane. First names seem more appropriate in a situation like this."

When she stepped inside, he shook her hand. His grip was warm and firm. Something about him was sturdy, and she knew she had an ally if she needed one.

Jana met the parents and learned the lost child's name was Amy. They showed her a picture of the blond four-year-old with a smile that could bring sunshine to anyone's day. As Jana studied the picture, she instantly felt cold. Especially her cheek. She sensed darkness, brush, dampness, and saw four boulders stacked on top of each other. They looked unsteady, but Jana had the feeling they'd stood that way for decades.

"Get me something of Amy's. A shirt, sweater..."

As soon as she held the small yellow sweater, her hands tingled with warmth, and she whispered, "She's okay. Tired and cold, but okay. Shane, I need someone familiar with the area to go with me."

"I know the canyons."

"Should we notify one of the police search parties?"

"No. I have a cellular. If we find her, I'll call it in."

"All right. I work better when someone's not breathing down my neck."

Shane smiled and grabbed a jacket hanging over the back of a kitchen chair. "Is that a warning?"

She shook her head. "People get anxious in situations like this. I need the freedom to make mistakes."

He nodded. "Then let's get to it."

Amy's parents begged Jana to let them go along. But she advised them to wait at the house in case the search parties found Amy first.

Shane and Jana slipped out the back door. She'd worn jeans and a sweatshirt of Adam's he'd loaned her, knowing night in the canyons would be cool. Besides flashlights, each of them carried a blanket. They didn't talk. It was as if Shane knew instinctively that Jana needed to concentrate. They crossed a street that led to wooded areas and hills. Jana took one of the paths worn in the brush. After about a quarter of a mile at a fork in the path, she stopped and breathed and listened. She didn't hear the other search parties.

"They already combed this area," Shane said matter-of-factly.

"In the dusk," she murmured. "They missed her."

"I don't like the sound of that. Is she hurt?"

"I don't think so. I don't get that sense. But she is lying on the ground."

"Where to?"

"An area where there are boulders, lots of boulders, and brush."

"Up to the left."

She nodded. "That's what I'm getting. I wanted to make sure."

After they trekked another quarter of a mile, they came to a level clearing. Jana held the sweater, stared into the moonlit night and let vibrations flow. "Four boulders, Shane. Stacked like a tower. She's behind them, curled into a ball in the brush."

"This way. I know the spot."

Jana heard the anticipation in his voice, the hope and an element of surprise that maybe she could really find this child. After a short distance, the shadow of the boulders fell across sparse brush. She hugged the small sweater to her, feeling Adam's sweatshirt against her skin. The thought of him and his daughters wasn't a distraction. Lead by an inner radar, she strode toward the boulders with confidence.

Circling them, she found a small cavelike aperture. Flashing her light inside, she saw Amy, curled against the dropping temperature, her thumb in her mouth. Jana handed Shane the flashlight and dropped down on the ground with the blanket. When she held the little girl in her arms, Amy's arms went around her neck. And as

Amy asked sleepily, "Mommy?" tears came to Jana's eyes.

She was glad she'd agreed to go back to Adam's. She wanted to be with him and his daughters. Now and always.

Chapter Nine

The information Adam had fed into the computer spewed from the laser printer. As always, work was the solution for insomnia. He'd stayed up until midnight, then turned in. He couldn't sleep knowing Jana was out in the canyons somewhere. He thought back over the time since he'd met her. Then he examined his reactions over the past week—gratitude to Jana for finding Karla and Stacey, his daughters' acceptance of Jana in their lives, his desire for her that he couldn't seem to banish, his jealousy on the plane, his overreaction to Jon's advice, his need to have Jana near him as often as possible.

None of it made sense except the gratitude. The rest—the emotions, the needs—were facets of himself he didn't know. He'd never felt jealousy with Leona. He'd never wanted to be around her twenty-four hours a day. No, it didn't make sense.

Commotion outside interrupted Adam's analysis. He'd been listening for Jana's car since he'd gotten up at one and settled in his office. Glancing at the clock, he saw that it was 1:30 a.m. So what was all the noise?

He went to the window and spied at least five sets of headlights. "What the—?"

Hurrying to the front door, he didn't bother to button the shirt he'd thrown on with his jeans. As he pulled the door open, Jana ran up the steps, looking exhausted and upset.

"I'm sorry, Adam. I didn't realize they were following me until I turned into the hills. I don't know how to get rid of them."

Before he could open the screen door to let Jana inside, two men and a woman with microphones jammed the steps. The woman called, "We know your name's Jana Kellerhern and you led the searchers straight to Amy. We'll get the story from someone. It might as well be your version."

Another said, "I have connections at the PD. Either you tell us or my source will."

"What does Shane Walker have to do with it? Are you working with him?" a third reporter practically yelled.

Bright, glaring lights shone on both of them. Adam came outside and stood in front of Jana, protecting her from the barrage. "This is private property, and you're trespassing."

"Whose property is it?" the woman asked, not taking his warning seriously.

"Turn off the lights and cameras and I'll talk to you."

"Adam, you don't have to do this," Jana said at his side. "I don't want them to wake up Karla and Stacey, so I'll do whatever it takes—"

Jana had said from the beginning that her gift caused a three-ring circus, and now he believed her. He held up his hand to the reporters as the lights went off. "Give me a minute with Ms. Kellerhern." When one of the lights went back on, Adam said angrily, "If you don't give us a few minutes, you won't get anything from either of us."

Someone turned the light off, and the reporters backed away for the time being.

Adam draped his arm around Jana's shoulders, aware of how she fit into his body, aware of her hair brushing his bare chest and arousing him even in this chaotic situation. He turned her toward the porch, his head bent close to hers, as he concentrated on her words rather than her scent and the feel of her beside him. "Tell me what happened."

She did, as briefly as possible.

"You're wonderful. You know that?"

She tipped her head up and gave him a weak smile. "No. This is just something I can do that other people can't." She glanced over his shoulder. "Now, how do we get rid of them?"

He tweaked her nose. "How do you feel about giving a press conference tomorrow?"

"A press conference? Adam, I'm not a celebrity. And if I give a press conference, I'll lose my privacy altogether."

Adam tilted his head toward the reporters. "I'm afraid you've lost it by finding Amy. At least at a press conference you can control the circus. I'm sure Shane will support you and maybe the little girl's parents would answer some questions. It would take some of the focus away from you if that's what you want."

"Of course that's what I want. I hate this." She sighed. "But maybe it's time not only to face reporters but my future, too. All right. Let's tell them."

Adam squeezed her shoulder. "Go inside and get ready for bed. I'll take care of everything." He saw she wanted to argue with him, she wanted to stand on her own, but she was simply too tired.

Finally, giving him a nod, she went inside, but stood behind the screen door. He knew she'd wait there until he handled the reporters, until she was sure she didn't need to speak with them herself. Jana Kellerhern was one independent lady, and he admired her for it.

In the morning the click of the bedroom door awakened Jana. She opened her eyes and ran her hand through her hair as Adam came in carrying a tray. He looked better than the scrambled eggs, bacon and toast on the breakfast plate. His white polo shirt was open at the neck, revealing his chest hair. The navy shorts hugged his hips and flat stomach. She hardly remembered his good-night last night, or rather earlier this morning. But she couldn't forget the brief touch of his lips on her forehead before she'd closed the bedroom door.

"What time is it?"

"Ten."

She pushed herself up on her elbows. "Adam, my goodness. Why didn't you wake me? I have to call Shane—"

"I called him. He'll be here for the press conference. So will Amy's father. I also told Harriet you wouldn't be in and you'd get in touch with her to let her know what's going on. I didn't know how much you'd want me to tell her." Setting the tray on her lap, he sat beside her hip, his thigh brushing hers under the sheet.

She tried to ignore the sensation of being so close, so intimate. "I'll probably tell her everything at this point. If it's going to be on the news... What about Karla and Stacey? I hate to involve them in all this commotion."

"They'll be fine. I'll tell Karla she can play in her room or watch from the staircase. I'll hold on to Stacey. All you're going to do is give a statement and answer a few questions."

"You make it sound so simple."

He grinned. "It is. Now drink your juice and eat your breakfast."

"With you watching?" she teased.

He snitched one of the four slices of bacon and took a bite while his eyes lingered on her mouth, the pulse at her throat and finally on the yellow T-shirt she'd worn to bed. "I like watching you."

She felt her cheeks get hot. If the girls weren't in the house, it would be so easy to turn back the sheet, invite him in....

He must have guessed the direction of her thoughts because he leaned across the tray and gave her a slow, lingering kiss that woke every cell that hadn't already awakened just from the sight of him.

When the coffee cup on the tray rattled, he broke the kiss and stood. "I'd better get back downstairs before Stacey smears jelly over everything besides the toast." His words were raspy as if toast and jelly were the last thing on his mind.

The taste of bacon from his lips and tongue made her hunger for much more than breakfast. "Thank you, Adam. I can't remember the last time I had breakfast in bed. And last night with the reporters—"

He dismissed her thank-you with a frown. "I owe you. Anything I can do to help, I'll do."

He owed her? Is that how he saw this? As a payback? She suddenly lost her appetite. "You don't owe me anything. I told you before that I use my gift because I have it, not to get payment of any kind."

"Bringing you breakfast *wasn't* payment." His voice held irritation, and his jaw set stubbornly.

"Then what was it?" she prompted.

"Something I felt like doing because I thought you'd appreciate it."

"I do."

"Good." He went to the door and stopped. "We should go over your statement to the press. I'll see you downstairs after you're dressed."

Jana nodded. "I won't be long."

He closed the door with a thud.

She laid her head against the pillow and felt like crying. Adam wasn't about to admit to any feelings, even if he had them. Sighing, she picked up her juice and took a few sips. All of a sudden, she shivered. A picture popped into her head, the same picture she'd gotten in France—Adam embracing Leona.

What did it mean?

Adam's living room looked more like a movie set than a place to relax. But that could be expected with microphones and lights and cameras. He winked at Karla, who waved from the staircase, and hitched Stacey higher in his arms as she watched the cameraman in fascination. Out of the corner of his eye, he spotted Jana rubbing her palms on her jeans, then making sure the collar of her red blouse lay in a proper V at her throat.

Shane placed one of his large hands on her shoulder. "Relax. You did something good, Jana. Just give them the facts."

"It's not so much the press conference I'm worried about. It's the aftermath."

Adam wondered what the aftermath would be. This morning in the bedroom... He wasn't sure why his gratitude had upset her. And he wasn't sure why her question about his motives had angered him. Everything about this situation with Jana was complicated. Even now, watching Shane's hand on her shoulder, Adam wished it were his hand there. He couldn't be jealous of Shane Walker. The private investigator was no predatory wolf.

One night when Adam feared he'd never find his daughters, he and Shane had gone to a club for a few drinks. Shane had listened to Adam, Adam had listened to Shane. The P.I. worked more hours than Adam used to and avoided getting involved with women with a vengeance. Yet, at this moment, Shane Walker was looking at Jana with gentle eyes. Adam couldn't help but wonder if she brought out the best in everyone she met.

At one o'clock precisely, Shane commandeered the microphone, announcing that he would explain what transpired the night before. Afterward he, Amy's father and Jana would be open to questions from the reporters. A communal gasp escaped the crowd when Shane explained he'd called Jana in on the case because she was a reputable psychic. No sooner had he finished his statement when the press zeroed in on Jana.

"How long have you worked with P.I.'s?"

"What was your first case?"

"When did you realize you had some magic power?"

The questions bombarded Jana, and Adam was ready to chase the whole entourage out of his house when she held up her hand for silence. In a soft but firm voice, she told them how she'd been struck by lightning and how she'd first used her gift at age sixteen.

Adam listened intently. When they'd prepared her statement, she hadn't included this.

"I hid my ability until then. My best friend didn't come home one night. As soon as I held her scarf, I pictured a scene. Nancy had been in an accident. She'd hit a deer darting across the road and bumped her head on the steering wheel. I could picture the exact location where the police could find her."

Adam wondered why Jana had never told him about that first experience. Then he realized he'd never asked.

After fifteen minutes of questions, a few of which were directed to Amy's father and Shane, the rest to Jana, Adam went to the sofa where the three were seated and took the mike from Jana. "That's it, folks. You have plenty."

With a last flurry of questions and complaints, the reporters acquiesced to Adam's order. Shane shepherded Jana and Amy's father out to the patio as he and Adam had discussed before the press conference.

Adam had closed the door on the last camera technician when Karla asked from the stairs, "Can we go swimming when we get up from our nap?"

He had to smile. So much for the press making an impression on his daughter. "Sure." He tickled Stacey's stomach, and the toddler giggled as he carried her up the stairs.

After he settled the girls for their rest time, he slid open the door to the patio and saw Amy's father shaking Shane's hand. Then the man turned to Jana. "I can't begin to express how grateful me and my wife are to you. You saved Amy's life.''

"I was glad to be able to help."

"If you ever, ever need anything, just give us a call. Shane might not have mentioned it, but I run a travel agency. If you want to go anywhere, you call me and I'll get you the best discount I can. Agreed?''

She took the hand he extended and shook it. "Agreed."

Adam understood the man's gratitude because he felt the same way. If it weren't for Jana... He approached the group. "The coast is clear. Everyone left."

Jana glanced at her watch. "I have to go, too. I told Harriet I'd be there at four. I have to stop at my apartment and change..." She headed for the living room.

"Jana?" Adam's voice stopped her. "When do you get off work?"

"Nine."

"I'll call you."

"That's not necessary."

"I'll call you," he insisted again.

She looked as if she might protest, then she didn't. She said softly, "I'll talk to you later."

Adam had the feeling she was running away from him. He wanted to pull her back, but he didn't know how.

He called her at nine-fifteen. When she didn't answer, he dialed again at nine-thirty and again at ten. At ten-thirty, he was ready to call Shane and the police. But at eleven she answered, fatigue evident in her voice.

He tried to keep his anxiety from showing. "Are you all right?"

"I quit my job."

"Why?"

"I lost my freedom again. And it's worse here than back in Deep River. At least there, they're used to what I do."

"Jana, what happened?"

"The reporters did their homework. On the evening news they not only told the city what happened with Amy, but they told everyone where I worked. The scene at your house last night was mild. I had people lined up out the door to get manicures and hopefully a free psychic reading. Dammit, Adam, this is what I wanted to escape!"

He could hear the frustration and anger in her voice and he thought he discerned a hint of panic. "Is that why you're home so late?"

"No. I stopped taking customers at nine, but I had a few people on my tail. Maybe they were reporters. I don't know. So I drove until I lost them. Thank goodness I have an unlisted number. For all I know, they could be sitting outside my door. Shane got my number for you. I'm sure others can get it, too."

Adam rubbed the back of his neck and sank into the swivel chair at his desk. "I ran off a few reporters after you left. They haven't returned, probably because they know you're back at your apartment. All it takes is one nose at the right place, and they all follow. I feel responsible. If I hadn't pushed the press conference—"

She didn't let him finish. "It's not your fault. Finding Amy was news." There was no accusation in her tone, just the frustration of having to cope with all of it.

"Come stay here a few days until the hullabaloo dies down."

"No. I'll be fine. I just have to decide what I'm going to do next."

Disappointment filled him. Not only did he want to protect her, but he liked the idea of having her around. "You really quit your job?"

"I had no choice."

He knew she was desperately tired and needed to sleep. "Call me if you need me."

Jana didn't respond, and he suddenly wondered if she'd call Shane first. That was absurd. Wasn't it?

The next day, Adam tried to call Jana at least ten times, and each time her line was busy. What the hell was going on? He'd decided to drive over there with Stacey and Karla after supper when his doorbell rang. Leaving the girls in the kitchen, twirling spaghetti, he answered it.

Jana stood on his porch, overnight case in hand. "I decided to accept your invitation if it's still open."

"Of course it is." He took the bag from her hand and tugged her inside.

Her expression was anxious and tentative. "I didn't know where else to go. The wire services picked up the story. The phone rang off the hook all day. Writers wanting interviews. Would you believe someone wants to do a book? What is it about Los Angeles? In Deep River I was simply an oddity. Here, everything has exploded."

He'd never seen Jana frazzled, but she looked close to it now. Dropping the bag, he took her in his arms and held her. "You can stay here as long as you need to."

Rigid in his hold, she protested, "But they might get your phone number."

"We'll let the machine take all the calls. And if anyone sets foot on the property who shouldn't, I'll hire guards to run them off."

"Adam, I don't want to disrupt your life and Karla's and Stacey's."

Gazing into her eyes, he tried to reassure her. "You know the girls will be delighted you're here. This will die down, Jana. You just have to let it run its course."

Finally going limp, she laid her head on his shoulder and mumbled into his chest, "I hope you're right."

So was he.

With the answering machine monitoring calls for Jana and the others going through Adam's office, she found relief from the chaos. Now and then an odd reporter showed up, but for the most part the furor had died down. She could concentrate on simply hiding out and enjoying her time with Adam and Karla and Stacey. She had never really taken care of anyone but herself. Her relationship with Brian had been more of a dating courtship, and she now realized they hadn't been very close. Not in the way she and Adam were.

It seemed natural for her to get up in the morning, go downstairs and start breakfast. She was learning Adam's and Stacey's and Karla's likes and dislikes. Stacey was a picky eater. No syrup on her French toast. Butter on one slice. Karla soaked her toast with syrup and could eat two slices. And Adam. He used apple butter, no syrup and ate at least four.

They'd fallen into a routine. After breakfast, Adam worked in his office awhile. Jana spent time with the girls, teaching them crafts or taking them shopping, or to the park. She would prepare lunch, then as the girls rested, Adam would spend another hour or so in his office. In the late afternoon the four of them would swim, cook supper and afterward go for a drive or take a walk.

On the Fourth of July they'd watched fireworks burst into glory over the ocean.

In some ways it was like a vacation for Jana. She hadn't taken one since she'd graduated from college. But in others . . .

After Karla and Stacey went to bed, she and Adam would play Scrabble or cards. They competed, laughed, and Jana fell deeper in love. Adam's kisses were restrained, yet potent nonetheless, and Jana couldn't help but wonder what would happen if the girls weren't in the house.

On the fifth evening, she and Adam sat on the patio while Karla and Stacey played in the yard. Abruptly he folded the newspaper he'd been reading and laid it on the flagstone beside him. "Are you going to get another job?"

His question brought Jana back to reality with a jolt. She'd known the serenity of the past few days couldn't last. "I have to decide whether or not I'm going to stay in Los Angeles. I spoke to my mother last night and she told me one of her friends would like to buy into the craft shop. I could sell my interest. But I don't know if I'm ready to do that."

"I might have a temporary solution if you're not ready to sell out and need more time to decide. If Leona lets me keep the girls for the summer, I'd like you to stay and take care of them."

Her heart seemed to sink to her toes. She tried to read the expression on Adam's face, glimpse some emotion in his eyes. But she couldn't. "You want me to be your housekeeper?"

He frowned. "No, of course not. I'd have my usual cleaning lady come in. You'd do what you've been doing this week. Play with Karla and Stacey, teach them, make them breakfast and lunch—''

"You want a nanny."

"I want you."

But as what? her heart cried. As a lover, a housemate, a baby-sitter? She loved Adam with all her heart. She wanted to spend days with Karla and Stacey and time with him. But not as a paid employee! Dreams of his love, and a future, and nights in his arms grabbed at her heart. She didn't want to be his employee; she wanted to be his wife!

The doorbell rang. Adam swore and said, "I'll be right back. Think about it."

She'd hardly had time to absorb the extent of her love for Adam when he returned to the patio, Leona beside him. His ex-wife was saying, "So I decided to take an earlier flight out and here I am." When she saw Jana on the patio, she stopped. "Hello, again. Adam didn't tell me he had a guest."

Jana stood. All week she'd felt comfortable at Adam's house. Now she didn't. "Adam has let me stay here a few days as an escape. I'm sure he'll tell you all about it. If you'll excuse me, I have a few calls to make. I'll say good-night to Karla and Stacey and head up to my room."

Before either Adam or Leona could respond, Jana slipped off the lawn chair, gave each child a hug, then went inside. She didn't intend to watch Leona and Adam interact. She didn't intend to feel like a fifth wheel.

With a glance at Jana's closed bedroom door, Adam let Leona put the girls to bed. Afterward, he walked her to the front door. "They're glad you're back."

"But they're happy here with you, too."

"Did you hope they wouldn't be?"

Leona blushed and murmured, "It's hard for me to let go."

"You're their mother. Nothing will change that."

"They like Jana."

Karla and Stacey had told Leona about their day at Disneyland, the picnic with Jon, the past few days playing and shopping with Jana. "She likes them."

When he didn't say more and the silence stretched awkwardly, Leona said, "I've decided to let the girls stay with you for the summer. If that's what you still want."

Relief swept over him, and the tension that had coiled inside him since Leona had taken the girls finally dissipated. "I do. And I guess you should know I've asked Jana to take care of them for the summer if I have them. Do you have any objections?" They might as well get this hashed out now to avoid complications later.

Leona was quiet for a moment. "No. I watched Jana with them in France. She's very capable."

He heard the reservation his ex-wife wasn't articulating. "But?"

"I want to be able to see the girls often. I know this would be the perfect opportunity for you to take your revenge—"

"Do you really think I'd do that?"

She searched his face. "I suppose not. That's something Father would do."

Her comparison of him and Arthur Carrero had been one of the problems with their marriage. Leona had expected Adam to act like her father in most areas, yet she had wanted him to give her the time and attention her father had never given her. Mixed messages at best, mistaken expectations from the beginning. "I won't keep you from your daughters."

She looked relieved. "Actually I might be taking a few trips this summer if you have the girls."

Adam saw the sparkle in Leona's eyes that hadn't been there for a long time. "With Jean Watteau?"

She nodded. "He's thinking about moving his main office to L.A."

"I'd like to meet him sometime."

"I think you'd like Jean. It's funny, except for his background and his money, he's really not like Father, either. He's kind and playful..." She blushed again.

"I hope you find what you want, Leona."

"I think I have," she said softly. "What about you?"

"As long as I have my daughters near me, I don't need much else."

"Don't fool yourself, Adam. Men and women aren't that different when it comes to needing someone to love. You and I together—we just didn't work. Or maybe we didn't know enough to make it work. Me and Jean—everything's there. We know it when we're together. Don't close your heart, Adam. You'll never be happy if you do."

Maybe his heart had never been open and that's why his marriage to Leona hadn't worked. He'd have to think about that. But he wasn't ready to discuss his psyche with his ex-wife. They had never let each other get that close. Changing the subject, he suggested, "When Watteau's in town, give me a call. We can go to dinner."

She shook her head. "All right, we won't talk about your life. For an intelligent man, Adam, sometimes..." Then she smiled and did something she hadn't done in years. She hugged him. "Thank you for not punishing me for taking the girls."

He gave her a light squeeze and pulled away. "Punishing you would only punish them. We'll work out our differences for their sakes. Right?"

She smiled. "Right."

Jana came out of her room when she heard Adam and Leona go downstairs. Karla and Stacey's door was open, and she peeked inside. Stacey lay without covers, her legs tucked up to her stomach, her arms clutching Muffin, her furry toy cat. Karla was sprawled on her stomach under a sheet, one arm hanging over the side of the bed. Both looked fast asleep.

Pausing at the top of the stairs, Jana heard Leona's and Adam's voices but couldn't distinguish what they were saying. She didn't need to hear them because she saw Adam embrace Leona. Leona's satisfied smile said more than any words, and Jana knew what she had to do.

Chapter Ten

Fifteen minutes later when Adam knocked on Jana's bedroom door, she was ready to face him and called, "Come in."

He opened the door and took in what she was doing with one swift appraisal. "Going somewhere?"

She pulled a blouse from the closet. "It's time."

"It wasn't time a few hours ago. What brought this on?"

Avoiding his gaze, she took the blouse from the hanger and folded it. "I called Mr. Mimoto, the manager of my building. He told me no one's hanging around anymore."

"That's because you're not there. If you go back..."

With a gentle flop, the blouse joined her folded shorts. "I'll deal with it. Mr. Mimoto did say I have stacks of mail."

"So, you're not accepting my offer?"

His offer. The one that made her realize where she stood in his life. "No. I can't. I could be here today and gone tomorrow. That's not good for the girls."

"Are you going back to Indiana?" Adam's tone was even and controlled, betraying no emotion.

"I'm not sure. First, I have to see what all the mail is about and go through messages I've ignored. Then, I'll decide."

"Jana?"

She stopped rearranging the clothes already packed in her suitcase and met his gaze, looking for hope, wishing for a sign from him that said he wanted her in his life. "I'll say goodbye to Karla and Stacey tomorrow after breakfast."

"You make it sound so final."

"I've got to get my life in order, Adam."

"I guess everybody has to do that. Leona is letting the girls stay here for the summer."

"Good. I know that's what you wanted. I'm glad you could iron out your differences." He didn't deny it, and Jana wondered what other differences he and Leona had ironed out.

He came toward her and stopped close enough to touch her, close enough that he could probably hear the pounding of her heart. "I'll miss you."

She fought the emotion that pressed against her throat. "I won't be that far away."

"Maybe after you have a few days to make decisions, we can have dinner."

"Maybe."

He turned and went to the door. "I'll see you at breakfast."

She nodded because tears were too close to the surface for her to speak. When the door closed behind him, she looked at the open suitcase and felt pain deeper than her heart, deeper than her soul. Love hurt so much.

Two cartons of letters sat beside Jana at her desk. She flipped open another one and read the story of a woman who wanted Jana's help to make contact with her deceased husband. The phone rang. Jana let her machine take it, hoping it was Adam. But it wasn't. It was a message from yet someone else who wanted to make an appointment for a reading. If Jana hoped leaving Adam's house would make him realize he loved her, she was wrong. She hadn't heard from him in four days.

An hour later when her doorbell rang, she went to the peephole expecting to see Harriet or Mr. Mimoto. She saw Adam. Her heart raced, her fingers tingled and she felt a smile well up from inside her. When she opened the door to him, he smiled, too.

"The place is a mess," she said as he stepped into the living room.

Letters lay open in piles on her desk. She'd spilled some, lifting them from the carton on the floor to the blotter. The phone rang again. Its sound came from the unit in the kitchen, not the one on the end table in the living room. "I'm letting the machine take them all," she said as she waved at it.

"You look tired." Adam's voice melted over her like a soothing balm.

"I am tired. But if I don't keep up with the correspondence, it will pile up."

"You need a secretary."

"I have to do it myself."

"Jana, you can't do it all yourself. You'll run yourself ragged. Especially if you decide to help any of these people. You have to think about yourself and your limits."

"You don't know what it's like to have a talent so many people seem to need!"

"You can't help everyone."

"Maybe I have to try."

He shook his head and came closer to her. "Maybe you give too much. Maybe you have to learn how to say no."

"That's much harder to do than it sounds."

Reaching out, he caressed her cheek. "Karla and Stacey want to know when you're coming over again. They miss you." He paused for a moment. "*I* miss you."

The huskiness in his voice, the silver sparks in his blue eyes, made her tremble as much as the heat of his fingers on her face. "I miss you, too."

Adam tugged her into his arms and lowered his mouth to hers. He didn't hold back as he locked his hands at her back and drew her tight against him. Before, he'd restrained himself. Before, he'd been in control. Before, he'd given and taken with a limit. In this kiss, no limits existed.

His lips promised erotic pleasures she'd only dreamed about as he nibbled and sucked and explored. His hands slipped under her tank top and when they met bare skin, he growled deep in his throat and thrust against her. She met his thrust with the same desire. His kiss and touch brought to life her fantasies, ignited her desire until it burned as brightly as his, seduced her into believing this was everything she wanted and needed.

His tongue slid deep within her mouth, and as he rocked his hips provocatively against hers, she knew she wanted to be one with him. She caressed his neck and glided her fingers through his hair. He groaned, angling his head for more of her kiss. Breaking away, he slipped her top up her body and over her head. She didn't think about protesting. She didn't think at all.

With abandon she'd never felt before, she unbuttoned his shirt quickly and ran her hands up his chest, glorying in his chest hair erotically brushing her palms. He was hot and hard. She leaned into him, bringing her lips to his skin. She kissed him softly, then rubbed her cheek against him.

Adam sucked in his breath and held her head there. His heart pounded under her ear, his breathing was deep and fast. He unhooked her bra and touched her shoulders, holding her away from him. The bra dropped to the floor.

He stared, the look in his eyes as potent as his kiss. Swooping her up into his arms, he carried her to her bedroom. He kissed her again as he lowered her to the bed and came down beside her. Caught up in their passion, Jana locked her arms around his neck. The room spun, her world tilted, all she could smell and think and feel was Adam.

As he stretched out on top of her, the flaps of his shirt lay on either side of her. His chest against her breasts, his hips cradled so perfectly against hers, brought a moan from her soul.

He pulled away and raised himself on his elbows. "This is right, Jana. I need you, you need me."

Need. Need. Need.

The word echoed along with the reverberating tingles of excitement. Adam needed her. But she didn't just need Adam, she loved him. How long would his need last? One night, a month, a year? Until he found someone he needed more? Until he solved his differences with Leona?

She opened her eyes and stared at him, hoping to see more than need, hoping to see love.

"Jana? What's wrong? I have protection if you're worried..."

Her breath caught in her throat. "You planned this?"

"No, I didn't plan it. I hoped."

She managed to control her voice. "What's the difference?"

He pushed himself to his side and studied her carefully. "You and I both know this passion has been building between us since the moment we met. I hoped with Leona spending the evening with the girls, we'd have the time and the opportunity to... pursue it."

His hesitation was the giveaway. "You can't say it, can you?"

"Say what?"

"That you hoped we'd have the time and opportunity to make love. Because that's what I'd be doing, Adam. Loving you."

He looked stunned, then angry. "We're talking about sex, Jana. Sex. I never said anything about love."

Tears burned her eyes. "I know you didn't. But I did. I love you, Adam. Believe me, I didn't want to. I've been hurt before. But it happened anyway. And I can't make love to you without loving you."

Pushing himself up against the headboard, he shook his head. "Love. I'm not sure I know what it is. Why do you want to complicate this? Why can't we just—?"

"Have sex? You say that's what you want. But I think I've gotten to know you pretty well. Can you have sex with me and not feel anything?"

"I'll feel something, all right," he snapped. "Arousal. Climax. Satisfaction. Gratitude that you found my daughters."

"If that's true, I don't belong in this bed with you." With her top half naked, she now felt self-conscious. Hopping out of bed, she reached for the robe laying over her chair.

"Jana, you know my history. I made a commitment, and I was a bad father and a lousy husband."

He was holding on to the past, and she suspected the reason—he still had feelings for Leona. And if he didn't... "You're a good father now. You're caring and compassionate. But it doesn't matter what I believe. It's what you believe that matters." Somehow she'd fallen into the same pattern with Adam that she'd fallen into with Brian. She'd given to him and his daughters, hoping the feelings would be returned.

The words he'd used earlier came back to her. *You have to think about yourself and your limits.* Suddenly she knew what she had to do for both of them. "I'm going back to Indiana."

The silence was louder than the backfire of the truck outside her window. "When?"

Thank goodness the apartment had come furnished. Thank goodness she only had to pack her clothes and books, ship home the box of letters and she'd leave no trace. "As soon as I can arrange it."

"I see."

No, he didn't see. That was the problem. She held her breath, waiting for him to ask her to stay, hoping the thought of her leaving would open his eyes. But then, maybe she was wrong. Maybe he didn't feel anything but desire and gratitude. Maybe he wanted to go back to Leona.

Adam swung his legs over the side of the bed and buttoned his shirt. "So much for the evening I planned."

It could have been a wonderful evening. It could have been...

He added, "I'll tell Karla and Stacey you said good-bye."

She'd like to tell them herself, but it would be too difficult. She cared too much. And she couldn't bear to see Adam again. Not after tonight.

He stood and walked to her side of the room. "I'll let myself out."

Please ask me to stay! Tell me there's a chance.

He didn't hear her heart. At the doorway he said, "Goodbye, Jana."

She couldn't say the words, just as she couldn't believe he was leaving without even trying to persuade her to stay. She didn't need her sixth sense to understand the meaning of that. He didn't love her. In fact, he didn't even desire her enough to ask her to stay.

Without another word, he left. When she heard her apartment door close, she crumpled up on the bed and dropped her head into her hands. She'd mend. She'd heal. She'd find a way to help others that didn't hurt her.

Tears dripped down her cheeks, and the first sob broke loose.

Two evenings later, Jon opened his door to Adam. "You look like hell."

Adam didn't respond and stepped inside.

Jon took another appraisal. "Scotch or coffee?"

"Coffee."

"Where are Karla and Stacey?"

"They're spending the night with Leona."

"So why aren't you out somewhere with Jana?"

"Jana's out of the picture."

"What happened?"

"Nothing happened," he muttered.

"I know you, Adam, and—"

He swore forcefully. "Everybody thinks they know me."

Jon arched his brows.

"Sorry. I shouldn't take my frustration out on you."

His friend motioned Adam to the kitchen. "Let's get that coffee."

Adam wasn't used to talking about personal stuff. He'd shared more with Jana than he ever imagined he could. Why? What about her made her trustworthy? But the real question screaming in his gut was—why did he feel as if the bottom of his world had dropped out? He sank onto a chair at the table.

Jon poured two mugs of coffee and sat across from him. "Did you and Jana have a fight?"

There was no point denying anything to Jon. "She's going back to Indiana." Mowing his hand through his hair, he stood and paced the kitchen. "She probably intended to go back all along."

"Why shouldn't she go back?"

"Because..."

"Because of what?"

"I like Jana."

Jon took a sip of coffee and tilted his chair on the back two legs. "The same way you like a walk on the beach or a medium well-done steak?"

Adam's fuse blew and he swore. "Of course not. I need her smiles, I need her honesty, I need her giving nature."

"Did you tell her that?"

He stopped pacing. "No."

"Why not?"

"Because her mind was made up."

"You didn't ask her to stay?"

He slashed his hand through the air. "What's the point? She wants something I can't give her. She wants me to tell her I love her. I don't believe in love. Not the forever kind."

Jon righted his chair with a thump. "What about your daughters?"

"That's different. I'll love them till my dying breath," Adam vowed in a low voice.

Jon pinned Adam with a steady stare. "Think about how you feel about Karla and Stacey. Then think about how you feel about Jana. Are the feelings as strong? What happens when you think about the next few weeks, the next month, the next year without her?"

Jon's questions beat on Adam's heart one after the other. Adam turned toward the window, staring into the distance as he tried to answer them. He'd never felt anything as strong as what he felt for his daughters until Jana came along. Just as with them, he wanted to protect her, care for her, hold her, talk to her. Mixed with that was the elemental desire that could bring him to his knees. Is that why he couldn't recognize his feelings? Because Jana seemed to have some power over him and he was fighting it?

His life changed when she walked into a room. It was brighter, filled with hope, more exciting. He didn't want to imagine life without her. Was this love? Did he love her?

Jon broke the silence. "Did you know Jana was involved with a divorced man before?"

Adam swung around. He had never asked Jana about her past. Why? *Because you didn't want to face the jealousy you'd feel.* "No, I didn't know. How do *you* know?"

"That day you were here for the picnic. She was pretty upset after you snapped at her. She didn't say much, just that the man reconciled with his ex-wife. She did mention he'd had a son she'd gotten close to."

"She doesn't think that Leona and I will get back together, does she?"

"It's on her mind."

"That's ridiculous!"

"You know that. Does Jana?"

Adam stuffed his hands into the pockets of his slacks and didn't answer. "I'm going for a walk on the beach." Heading for the door, he paused at the threshold. "You know, you would make a damn good lawyer." He didn't wait for his friend to respond but strode toward the stone steps.

The beach stretched before Adam, an endless ribbon of sand washed constantly by the fingers of waves. He walked fast as if someone were chasing him. The walk broke into a run, and the soles of his leather shoes slapped the shore. He didn't care if he ruined the shoes, he didn't care if the salt water sprayed his shirt; he only cared about escaping the pain in his chest that seemed centered in his heart. He ran faster...harder. The pain wasn't physical. It came from the thought of Jana flying away from L.A., away from him....

You love her.

You love her.

You love her.

The words came from a voice inside of him that he'd ignored, denied, closed his heart to. He slowed and then stopped short.

"I love her." It came out raspy and got lost in the air he had to gulp in from his wild sprint. He took a few more deep breaths.

"I love her," he said again to the ocean, to the wind, to the pain in his heart.

The pain lessened just a bit.

Was it too late to say the words to Jana? Would she believe him? Why couldn't he have realized it sooner?

The answer was as obvious as the sweat on his brow. His upbringing, past mistakes, good old-fashioned fear had kept him from seeing it. Oh, he'd felt love all right. But he'd denied it. Jana had given to him freely—her time, her gift, her compassion, her acceptance and her love. Just like everyone else, he'd taken advantage of her giving nature, appreciating it, but not giving anything back. He'd been more enthralled with the chemistry between them than recognizing the fact that he loved her. And now it might be too late.

The other night, he'd seen the hurt in her eyes. He'd felt the bond between them shattering. Locked in a cage of self-doubt and denial, he'd left her. Jon's questions had pried open the windows of his heart and soul. Jana could read his heart if he opened it to her. And he wanted to do that.

Staring out at the ocean, the immensity of it, he now realized he and Jana couldn't box forever, couldn't own it, couldn't even understand it. But they could believe in it and they could touch it—if they loved each other, if they gave to each other, if they listened to each other. He wouldn't make the same mistakes. He'd learned how to be a good father, and he could learn how to be a good husband. If Jana was willing to give him the chance.

And if she'd already flown back to Deep River?

He'd go after her.

Adam had never done anything as crazy or impulsive. He climbed the outside steps to a second-floor apartment in Deep River, Stacey in his left arm, Karla holding tight to his right hand. He knew he was playing dirty by bringing his daughters, but at this point he was ready to use whatever ammunition he could. After his run on the beach, he'd gone straight to Jana's apartment in L.A. But the manager had told him she'd left.

Adam had never felt such a weight on his heart...until this morning when his plan had come together. He'd packed a few things for the girls and himself, chartered a plane and here they were. Karla and Stacey hadn't slept during the trip because they were too excited about seeing Jana again.

Wrapping her arms around Adam's neck, Stacey asked in a sleepy voice, "See Jana now?"

"I hope so, honey. Her lights are on. That's a good sign she's home and still up."

Karla tugged on his hand. "Do you have her present?"

"In my pocket."

At the door, Karla asked, "Can I ring the bell?"

"Go ahead. Ring it two times."

Karla grinned and did just that.

Adam heard the click of the lock. His stomach churning, his chest tight, his thoughts somewhere between hopeful and panicked, he waited. As Jana opened the door, he froze.

Her hair was mussed, her cotton robe had slipped over one shoulder, her eyes looked red-rimmed as if she'd been crying. All he wanted to do was take her in his arms. But that's what had gotten him into this mess. First, he'd tell her how he felt if it killed him.

"Adam! Karla and Stacey! What are you doing here?" Jana tried to shrug her robe over her shoulder.

"We came to visit," Karla explained.

Jana bent over and hugged the four-year-old. When Stacey lifted her arms to Jana, she took the little girl, gave her a kiss and carried her inside.

Adam wanted to say so much. But for now he settled on, "They've had a full day and are pretty beat. Can we tuck them into a bed?"

Jana met his gaze squarely. "I only have one bed."

"That's all right. You and I will probably be up talking all night, anyway."

Jana's cheeks grew rosy, and she seemed to be at a loss for words.

Adam went back to the car for the suitcase and unpacked the girls' nightclothes. After Karla and Stacey had brushed their teeth, drank sips of water from glasses Jana set on her night table and snuggled into the pillows, Jana covered them with a sheet. Stacey held out her arms for a last good-night hug for both Jana and Adam.

Karla asked Jana, "Are you gonna come home with us?"

Adam kissed his daughter's forehead. "While you're sleeping, Jana and I will talk about it."

Jana gave him an odd look as she said good-night to the girls one last time. With her shoulders squared and her back as straight as any military officer's, she went to one of the chairs in the small living room and perched on the edge. "Why did you come?"

Frustrated because the right words eluded him, Adam crossed to her chair and looked down at her. "I don't know how to do this. I don't know the right things to say. I only know I need you in my life."

"If you're saying this so I'll be the girls' nanny for the summer—"

"I don't want a nanny. I want you to be my wife. I love you, Jana. Will you marry me?"

She looked stunned beyond belief. "Just a few days ago you told me you didn't know what love was!"

"I was wrong. I had a talk with Jon and he made me see everything I'd been denying."

"He could, but I couldn't?"

Adam heard the hurt in Jana's voice, the pain of his earlier rejection of her love. He knelt down in front of her. "My feelings for you were so strong, so powerful, they blinded me to the truth. Jon managed to make me face it. I love you, Jana. And I want to be the man who gives you a lifetime of love."

"But what about Leona? I saw you hugging her."

He took both Jana's hands in his. "Leona hugged me. But it was an affectionate, maybe-we-can-be-friends hug. That's all. She's very much in love with her French businessman who is moving his headquarters to L.A."

Jana gazed at Adam with wide brown eyes that mirrored her thoughts—she still wasn't sure of the depth of his feelings. He released her hands and gently cupped her face between his palms. Reaching into his heart, opening it wide for her to see, he repeated, "I love you, Jana. Will you marry me?"

Tears welled up in her eyes as the truth of his words washed over her. "Yes, I'll marry you."

He scooped her into his arms, bringing her down on the floor with him. As he cradled her in his lap, he kissed her with the same fervor and depth of feeling that had emanated from his proposal. He held nothing back and neither did she.

When he came up for air, he muttered, "Some proposal." Reaching into his pocket, he pulled out a tiny box and lifted the lid. A solitaire diamond nestled against black velvet. "Karla and Stacey helped me pick it out."

"Oh, Adam. It's beautiful!"

He slipped it onto her finger. Tears glistened in her eyes, and he tilted his forehead against hers.

Jana brushed her fingers along the edge of his jaw. "Adam, I'll never try to take Leona's place with Karla and Stacey."

"You'll have your own place in their hearts." He felt Jana's brow wrinkle against his and could tell something was bothering her. "Jon told me you were involved with a divorced man before. Sometime I'd like you to tell me about that as well as every other little detail of your life before I met you. Is there anything I can do or say to reassure you that Leona is my past and you're my future?"

She leaned away. "You're a man of your word, Adam. I know that. If you say Leona is your past, I believe you."

Jana's faith in him was one of her most precious gifts to him. He kissed her again, knowing he'd do everything in his power to be worthy of it.

Jana broke away this time and still looked worried.

"What's wrong, sweetheart?"

"Adam, I have to use my gift to help people. Can you accept that? I have to travel sometimes . . ."

"Do you have a problem with my work? I have late meetings. I might miss supper."

"I understand, but—"

"Then I can understand the demands on your time. Are you going to keep your interest in the craft shop?"

She smiled—a full-blown, free, radiant smile. "Not if I'm going to live in L.A. with you."

He squeezed her tighter into his chest. "You're definitely going to live in L.A. with me."

Gazing at him with the depth of love overflowing from his own heart, she requested softly, "Say it again."

He knew exactly what she meant. "I love you."

She stroked his jaw. "I love you, too."

Adam bent his head to her lips once more. He'd reached for his star and found more joy and more love than he ever could imagine. Thanks to Jana. Thanks to her many gifts. Thanks mostly to her gift of love.

Epilogue

Fifteen months later

Jana waited for Adam on the patio. The pool lights glowed through the water, the blue radiance a romantic contrast against the black of night. She lit five tapered candles on the table next to the magnum holding sparkling grape juice.

When the sliding glass door opened, Jana's heart sped up as it always did whenever Adam was anywhere near. "Hi."

His gaze swept over the violet silk caftan that swirled in soft folds to her feet. "Hel-lo. Are we celebrating something?" He tugged down his tie, opened his shirt collar, then wrapped his arms around her.

She smiled and unknotted his tie, letting it hang loose around his neck. "Yes, we are. Remember Linda Renfrow?"

"The runaway teenager."

"Uh-huh. Shane and I found her today in Pasadena. Once she'd run away, she was too embarrassed to call home to say she'd made a mistake. Luckily we got to her before anything bad happened."

"You never get tired of finding people, do you?"

Not long after she and Adam were engaged, they'd invited Shane to dinner. She and Shane had talked at length about finding lost relatives as well as missing persons. They'd decided with Shane's skill and knowledge along with Jana's gift, they could make a difference. So she and Shane had formed a partnership and worked together ever since.

She'd never tire of reuniting loved ones. "I hope Linda and her mother can work out their differences. You should have seen Linda's face when she saw her mother at the door with open arms. And her mother... She was so happy."

Adam brushed Jana's cheek with his thumb. "You are, too. You're glowing."

"That's because I had a premonition."

His brows arched. He knew she didn't usually predict the future. "A vision of what a wonderful night we're going to have?"

"Not exactly."

"Are you going to tell me?"

She nodded. "I have to. You need to prepare."

"For something good?"

She decided to stop the twenty questions because she couldn't contain her excitement. "In eight months we'll be getting up at all hours for night feedings."

It took a moment for her meaning to register. "A baby?" He lifted her, swung her in a circle, kissing her at the same time.

When he set her down, she linked her arms around his neck. "I guess you're happy about it?"

"Ecstatic! Wait until Karla and Stacey hear."

"They'll be with us in June when the baby's born. Do you think they'll be jealous?"

"Maybe. But we'll deal with it. Just as we've dealt with everything else."

Jana had had a few run-ins with Karla when the little girl had defied Jana's authority, but through talking and laughing and negotiating with Leona and Jean, the four of them had managed to work out the situations.

"Do you know what I'd *really* like to do tonight?" Jana asked Adam coyly.

"What?"

"Skinny-dip."

His eyes sparkled with amusement, love and the passion that always burned brightly between them. "Why, Mrs. Hobbs! What will the neighbors think?"

"The neighbors won't know. We're surrounded by bushes and trees." She unfastened his second shirt button and then the third. "Well?"

He tipped her chin up. "I want to make love to you under the moon and stars and watch your eyes light up with the fire I feel every time I look at you or think about you."

She sighed because she felt so well and truly loved. "I love you, Adam."

"And I love you. Forever."

Jana nestled against him, reveling in the strength of his arms around her, the solid beating of his heart. The day they married, Adam had vowed to touch forever with her.

To touch forever.

What a wonderful vow, a vow they'd make every day of their lives. And keep. Together. For a lifetime and beyond.

*   *   *   *   *

The Darling Dad *series continues. Don't miss Jon's story, coming in September from Silhouette Romance!*

Take 4 bestselling love stories FREE

Plus get a FREE surprise gift!

**HE'S MORE THAN A MAN,
HE'S ONE OF OUR**

FATHER IN THE MAKING
Marie Ferrarella

Blaine O'Conner had never learned how to be a full-time father—until he found himself in charge of his ten-year-old son. Lucky for him, pretty Bridgette Rafanelli was willing to give him a few badly needed lessons in child rearing. Now Blaine was hoping to teach Bridgette a thing or two about love!

Look for *Father in the Making* in May, from Silhouette Romance.

Fall in love with our Fabulous Fathers!

R O M A N C E™

FF595

Continuing in May from

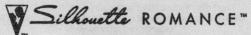

Silhouette ROMANCE™

by
Carolyn Zane

When twin sisters trade places, mischief, mayhem
and romance are sure to follow!

You met Erica in UNWILLING WIFE (SR#1063).
Now Emily gets a chance to find her perfect man in:

WEEKEND WIFE (SR#1082)

Tyler Newroth needs a wife—just for the weekend. And
kindhearted Emily Brant can't tell him no. But she soon
finds herself wishing this temporary marriage was for real!

Don't miss this wonderful continuation of the
SISTER SWITCH series. Available in May—only from

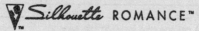

Silhouette ROMANCE™

SSD2